Trespass

and other stories

Trespass

and other stories

Judy Wilson

On the Brink Publishing
Hendricks, Minnesota

On the Brink Publishing
1572 State Highway 19
Hendricks, MN 56136

First Edition
Copyright © 2011 by Judy Wilson

All rights reserved. No part of this book may be used or reproduced in any manner whatsoever without written permission from On the Brink Publishing, except in the case of brief quotations embodied in critical articles and reviews.

Library of Congress Catalog Number: 2011908387
ISBN 978-0-615-48839-4

Printed on Acid Free Paper
Set in Palatino Linotype

The author gratefully acknowledges the following first publications of some of the stories included in this collection: "Cicada" in *Atlantic Monthly's Atlantic Unbound*; "Neverending" in *Mississippi Review Online* under the title "A Different Kind of Neverending," then reprinted in *Antietam Review*; the German translation of "A Different Kind of Neverending" in *Der Brennende Busch* titled "Eine andere Art Endlosigkeit;" "Silk" in *Urban Pioneer*; "Slivers," first as "Drive the Slivers Deep" in *Caprice* and reprinted in *The Texas Review* as "Slivers;" "Shrine" in *Front Porch Journal*; "Crossings" in *Farming Words Anthology*; "Substitute" in *Buffalo Carp*; "Seventh Day" in *SNReview*; "Doubt" in *The Oregon Literary Revew* under the title "Faith;" and "Trespass" in *Carve Magazine*.

Stories in this collection are fictions. Names, characters, places, and incidents either are products of the author's imagination or are used fictitiously. Any resemblance to actual events or persons, living or dead, is entirely coincidental.

FOR THOSE WHO FILL MY WELL
Bryon ¤ Jamie ¤ Jason ¤ Tiffiny ¤ and Bama

AND FOR MY MENTORS
Rick & Steve

Contents

Neverending ¤ 9

Slivers ¤ 33

Substitute ¤ 51

Cicada ¤ 63

Crossings ¤ 73

Shrine ¤ 101

Doubt ¤ 117

Seventh Day ¤ 129

Gone ¤ 149

Portrait ¤ 163

Silk ¤ 181

Adele X ¤ 197

Trespass ¤ 217

Neverending

The obstetrician turns the blood-streaked baby to face you, a presentation of sorts, his gloved hold almost mechanical. Beyond the tiny red contorted face—a son—the doctor smiles, his thick lips pressing against the surgical mask. You mumble, "my baby, my poor baby, poor, poor baby," and stretch to finger a slippery heel, minute toes. You'll remember later, much later, how peculiar that moment was, those words were. My poor baby. Of all the things to say, you'll think, but you'll shake it out of your head—a mere coincidence.

Your smiling balding husband leans against the delivery bed, rubbing your hair away from your forehead until it becomes irritating. You glance at him and smile. He's won his nine-month standing bet that it was a boy. The nurses take the baby to the far side of the room. You're not worried. They are taking care of him. The doctor tends to you, the afterbirth, the stitches. In his charming South African accent he tells you that he was paged from midnight mass—that he knew he had to hurry because you'd been slowly dilating for two weeks. He's pleasant and his hands move warm, quick. Many babies, he tells you, never once was he tardy. He draws the green sheet over your legs, pats your foot, and leaves you and your husband alone in the delivery room. The nurses had slipped out with the baby—when did they do that? you wonder.

"Why don't you rest?" your husband says and even though he's always been a gentle man, you've never seen his eyes that soft. "They'll probably bring the baby back in a minute. They're cleaning him up. I'll wake you," he says. You close your eyes against the chrome and lights of the room, just for a minute, you think.

You hear a different voice beside the bed. The pediatrician that you'd chosen stands beside you, wearing a gray Duke sweatshirt, no makeup, making polite conversation with your husband, but even in your daze, you know it's strange that she's been called to the hospital at three something in the morning. It has to be three something. She sees you've opened your eyes and begins her explanation—why she's there. Something a little odd with the baby, so they called her. The nurses panicked, she says. Nothing very serious, it could have waited until morning rounds. But the nurses, they were jumpy. So then she goes into the marrow of the story. The baby has a small opening in the roof of his mouth, a cleft palate, but not a very serious one. Didn't affect the lip or gum at all. Simple surgery to repair it, nothing to worry about. She's more concerned, she tells you, with the jaw—it's very undeveloped, doesn't give the baby much room for breathing unless he is lying on his stomach. The name for the anomaly, she says, is Pierre Robin Syndrome.

"Didn't you notice the jaw?" she asks. Haven't you seen the baby?"

You sputter, "For a second—I thought he looked fine, but I only saw him for a second."

Your husband withdraws from stroking your hair and sinks his elbows into the edge of the bed, his head turned toward your feet, and you can't make out his expression.

"I'm sorry, I thought you'd probably noticed and would be concerned. I'll have the nurse bring him in," she says. "It's nothing frightful, actually, just a bit odd."

An awkward quiet replaces her when she leaves the room. There isn't one single thing you have to say to your husband as he stares at the bed, fingering the sheets. Nothing at all that can be said or should be said. You wish he wasn't there, in fact, you wish he'd go away, before they bring the baby. You don't want him to see it, see him react to it. You don't want to worry about what he thinks of it, of you—of this, your ultimate screw-up.

Then the baby is in your hands—it's what you've wanted for months, for years, for almost half your life, to have your baby in your hands—and you squint, studying his face and you don't see it, the problem, the so-called oddity. Of course, he's screaming and his face is bunched up in the outburst and maybe that's the reason, you think, but when you look at your husband, you know—he sees it. And you blink the tears away and look again, trying to be totally objective, but you can't see it. The doctor hands you a medical glove and says, "Slip this on. You'll be able to feel the narrow cleft in his palate. I want you to feel it. I don't want you thinking that it's something worse than it is."

You prop the baby on your thighs while you work your right hand into the glove. Your fingertip seems too large as you slip it into his tiny warm mouth and you feel it, the small, V-shaped opening in the palate that widens toward the back. You smile because it's not so bad. Not so bad at all and the problem with the jaw, why, you can't even see it. They can, of course, you know that, but it can't be all that bad if *you* can't.

You tug the glove off and hold him to your cheek, breathe in his newborn smell and whisper to him, "Yes, we're going to fix it. We'll make it all better. It doesn't matter, no it doesn't," and his crying stops. In the corner of your eye you see your husband watching and you want to smack him—for the look on his face. You want to tell him "Go away, then, we'll be fine—you don't have to worry yourself with us." The doctor is saying, "The jaw will grow, correcting itself, but the cleft will require surgery in about a year."

"A year?" you say. "Why a year? Can't they fix it now—well, I don't mean right now. But a month, two?" You shift the baby to lie flat in your arms and suddenly he's struggling to breath and the crying resumes. And for the first time, you think you can see it, the lack of the lower jaw, a tiny face with an extreme overbite. The doctor tells you to put the baby on your shoulder, "Mustn't lay him on his back. His jaw settles and disrupts his air flow."

"Twelve to eighteen months," she says, "that's the age for this type of surgery. Besides, he's got the respiratory problem as well, and that could prove dangerous as far as anesthetizing." She has an irritating habit of carrying her blond hair behind her ears with her fingertips. Your husband has turned his back now, gazing toward a wall shelved with green sheets and small boxes, one hand in his pocket, his change, his keys, sounding through the room.

"You'll learn to care for him, to feed him, how to hold him and position him so that he doesn't experience too much distress. Tomorrow is soon enough. We'll let the nurses have him for now and get you in a room."

You kiss the baby's velvet cheek and, even though you want to keep him, pass him to the nurse.

Alone again with your husband, he turns, gives you a dry kiss on the cheek, a brush of his lips, and says, "I guess I'll go make the phone calls." He's tearful and you know when he gets away from you he won't go make the calls, not right away. He'll go sit in the car and beat his fist on the steering wheel. You know this—can see this happening. It's what you would do if you were he.

A buxom, gray-haired nurse wheels a clear acrylic bassinet into your room, your son on his tummy, legs and arms tucked beneath, like a fat, resting frog. Content. A blue card is taped to the foot of the bassinet—Tisdale Baby. The nurse raises the head of your bed. She's a noisy breather. "Did you get any sleep?" she asks, but doesn't wait for you to answer, and has yet to look at you. "Oh, you'll have to get used to that—not getting any sleep for a while. This little guy here is going to demand attention at the strangest hours," she says, pulling the covers away from the baby. "Yes, you'll be ready to snatch your hair out before he's done with you," she says chuckling, and you despise her. How dare she make assumptions? How dare she tell you how difficult it will be? She hasn't even looked at you, for Christ's sake, doesn't know the grief of even your first night. She lifts the baby, "C'mon, sleepy head," and hands him to you. His head is warm in your hand, his small, diapered bottom almost weightless in your other. He arches his back, arms stretching up, fist balled tight, and then the legs extend and you know these movements, have felt them from within. Instantly, like a sleeper who feels himself falling, he pulls his hands and feet back in, a horrible frown on his face, red lips quivering, and you harbor him to your chest, kiss his fuzzy head, explore the contours of his back with your fingertips, and his crying tapers off into earnest snorts. You lift him higher so that his head rests on your shoulder, his body molding to yours, and his breath warms your neck. A blue vinyl band circles his wrist matching the one on yours: Boy Baby # 1821. The nurse stands beside the bed, holding a strange looking bottle with a red, unnaturally shaped nipple.

"A cleft palate bottle," she says, flippant. She pushes her heavy glasses up along the bridge of her nose, sniffs, clears her throat, and says, "The bottle is wide and flat, squeezable," and she holds it in front of you, squeezing, her demonstration better suited for a six-year-old. You kiss your son on the cheek and run your finger around the curve of his ear.

"The nipple, you see, is also flattened and it has no hole at the tip. Instead, the hole is here," she holds it a foot and a half from your face, pointing to a hole on one side of the wide, flat nipple. "Your baby can't suck, so you'll squeeze the bottle for him off and on while he feeds. You'll have to learn to regulate the flow, the rhythm of the squeezes, to accommodate him—how fast he'll swallow, how often he'll pause—that sort of thing." She looks at you for the first time, pausing, as if she's asked a question and is waiting for a response. Annoyed, you nod for her to continue. "You want the hole to rest toward his tongue to prevent the milk from entering the sinus cavity. Take it slow at first, you don't want to flood his mouth with milk. He will have to learn this right along with you. You two will figure this thing out between yourselves." She filled the bottle then with formula from a small glass bottle, the kind the other babies would drink out of, you think. Holding the bottle toward you, she says, "Make sure you keep him propped up while feeding. And if you put him down in the bassinet, turn him on his tummy. Can't breathe otherwise." You take the warm bottle and she asks, "You want me to stay or would you be more comfortable if I left?"

You smile and say, "You can go. We'll be fine."

When she leaves, you put the bottle between your thighs to keep it from tipping and hold your son out to look at him. The jaw is visibly anomalous to you now, but the rest of him is so beautifully perfect. His eyes are large and round and dark and you know that once the jaw grows, those eyes will dominate. "What a handsome baby you are, do you know that? Do you know how much your mommy loves you, do you know?" Why am I whispering? you wonder. After all, he's real now. Still, you're conscious of not having anything significant to say as you sit staring at him, lifting the edge of his shirt—you want to see every part of him.

"Are you hungry, little man?" you ask, and settle his bottom on your legs, holding the back of his head, making sure to keep him propped. You pick up the bottle, your hand trembling, but you pretend you're confident because this is something you have to do. You have to feed the baby. They will send you home with him and you will have to feed him. Solo.

You make sure the hole faces the tongue as he takes the nipple in his mouth. You do nothing at first as he mouths it and then he's bunching his face up to cry so you lightly squeeze the sides of the bottle. There's no reaction of satisfaction from him and the nipple only seems to be muffling a wail. You take it out and look at it and at his screaming mouth. No sign of milk having been expressed. You take a deep breath and imagine the nurses huddling outside the door, listening to the baby scream, waiting to charge in. You touch the nipple to his gums and he takes it and as his lips close around it, you squeeze the bottle again, this time a bit harder. His crying ceases immediately, but he flails his arms out to the sides, his fingers extended. His head pushes back against your hand, eyes wide, and he's violently rigid. You pull the bottle away and see milk oozing from his nostrils and he looks like he's just been dunked under water. "Oh, God," you whisper, and the bottle falls from your hand. You wipe the milk away with your hospital gown, shaking, and tuck him over your shoulder, patting his back, listening for a breath, wishing he'd relax, wishing it was easier. Then you hear it—the caught breath—and it's followed by furious wails as he balls himself toward you. You're crying and rocking back and forth on the bed, your stitches feeling like thorns, and you know you should try again. But you rock and pat, rock and pat, cry, until the moment the pediatrician walks in and you hate her for just walking in. She's smiling and you know you must look like an idiot, rocking and patting while your baby screams away and the bottle lies leaking on the sheets between your legs.

"Not going so well?" she asks and takes the baby, the bottle, and puts the nipple in his mouth. With her first squeeze of the bottle, milk comes through the baby's nostrils. She wipes it away, gives him time to catch his breath, all the while smiling, and tries again. On the second squeeze, the baby swallows, and on the third and the fourth, yet with every squeeze he pushes his head backwards and his hands grasp the air, as if he's anticipating being overwhelmed again. After about twelve squeezes, she puts the baby on her shoulder, rubbing his back, and sits on the side of the bed. "He'll learn," she says, and now you love her. "I wanted to talk to you about the cleft—that's why I came in." She stands again with the baby and reaches to the wall, pulling a medical glove from its square holder. She hands you the glove and you say, "I felt it, remember?" She shakes her head, "It's different now." You slide your hand in the glove as she continues, "The skull and facial bones are compressed in the birthing process. Now that the bones are resuming their normal shape, the cleft appears somewhat larger. I wanted you to feel it then, and I think you should feel it now."

Again, you prop the baby against your thighs and slip a gloved finger in his mouth. "Jesus," you say as you feel the gap between the upper gums, "it's gone. He has no roof in his mouth." You can't imagine how it could be fixed. There is nothing there to work with. "Can they fix that?" you ask.

The pediatrician smiles, her fingers working her hair around her ear, "Heavens yes, you can build an entire mouth these days. But his feeding problems will be worse and he'll have trouble with his ears. Sometimes, too, babies that are born with one defect will have other defects that aren't so readily apparent. We'll have to watch." She rubs the baby's cheek with the back of her fingers. "He looks sleepy, mom."

You break off staring at her, your mind working on "defect" and "other defects," and remove the glove. You lift the baby to your chest and settle back on the pillows. His tiny knees press into you round and soft. You wonder if he's had enough to eat, but he's sleeping and you won't wake him. With your hand, you cover his back and you can barely feel his breathing. The pediatrician says, "We'll talk more later." You smile goodbye and watch her pull the door to, look over to the closed blinds at the long window, the sunlight forming a halo around the edges. A picture hangs on the wall near the window, the soft blur of pastels gone gray without light. Your baby warm on your chest, you wonder where your husband is.

The nurse comes back and stands over the bed. "How did we do?" she asks.

"Fine," you say and rub the hair around on the baby's head.

"I heard him fussing. Nothing wrong with his lungs, huh?" She's breathing as if she's been jogging.

"They all fuss, don't they? He was fine once he got started," you say.

She smiles, looking at the mostly full bottle on the bed-table, and reaches for the baby. Lifting him from your chest, she says, "We'll see if we can get some more in him for you. Not to worry."

The phone rings by your bed, sounding foreign, not at all like the one at home, and you hesitate before answering. It's your brother. "Congratulations. You finally did it." He's coughing sporadically—quick, dry coughs at the end of every sentence—a nervous tic.

"You know—right?" you asks.

"Yeah," he says and he's quiet.

You sit upright in the bed, your stitches tugging, burning, and say, "I want you to get some books from the library there at the university. Medical books. Anything you can find on cleft palate and Pierre Robin Syndrome."

"Can do," he says and he sounds almost happy. "I'll run by the library after my first class and bring them right out to you. About two hours. That okay?" Then, as an afterthought, he says, "Mom said tell you that she and Dad would be coming in this afternoon, most likely around two. I don't know where they're planning on staying. Didn't ask. Sis's probably."

"Wonderful," you say and your head pounds. You slip back down against the pillows.

When you hang up, you feel your exhaustion. Your husband made the calls—this you know at least. Maybe he went to work. You think about calling the house, but you don't want to move. You want to close your eyes and sleep, but you cry instead. You don't want to, you're tired of it, it's not a good cleansing cry anymore, just a draining, an endless grieving that you can't seem to control and it gives you no rest, no peace.

The next nurse that comes in with the baby is young and at least half way through her own pregnancy. She's efficient and polite, and you wouldn't mind, you think, if she wanted to talk to you, but she doesn't. The feeding works into a nightmare, milk consistently coming through the baby's nose, and you feel like a torturer. You try to remember how the pediatrician did it and to imitate her method, but he's fighting you on this. He refuses to swallow. The nice nurse comes back. "Did he take any for you?" she asks.

"Not enough to do any good, I'm sure," you say. "You might want to tell them in the nursery to try to get a bit more down him." You watch her handle him and she's comfortable with him, and careful, the way she wraps him and lays him in the bassinet. She'll be a good mother, you think.

"Well," she says, I'll see what they say, but they may tell me to bring him back to you. They're pretty busy down there. And he's a slow feeder, you know." She looks at her thin watch, writes on a metal-back tablet, and rolls the baby away.

Your brother comes in, two large books under his arm, sets them on the bed-table and kisses you on top of your head. You wish you'd combed your hair. Something. You haven't even considered it since you walked into the hospital, in proud labor. You imagine you must have been beaming then, smug with confidence in your pressed maternity dress. You'd taken the time to shower and shave your legs, for Christ's sake.

Your brother squeezes your arm, not realizing that it hurts you, that your muscles ache from hours of pulling at the handles of the delivery bed. You smile when he tells you he's seen the baby.

"He's a good looking baby. I was afraid to look at him at first. The way your old man talked. And the pictures in these books—I wasn't sure what I'd see." His eyes are honest, warm brown, and his cough is gone.

"He is wonderful, isn't he," you say and sit upright, running your hands through your tangles. He nods and you're glad to see him.

"So what's his name? Your old man said he doesn't know yet."

"Doesn't know yet? Of course he knows, there's never been any question," you laugh nervously. "He'll be Dean, Jr.—why the hell would he tell you that? Is that what he said, exactly? He doesn't know yet?" Your voice is too loud for the cramped hospital room.

"Actually, he didn't say anything. Just shrugged his shoulders," he says and imitates your husband, and even though your brother is young and physical, not at all like him, you can picture your husband doing this.

"Where is he? Do you know?" you ask. You notice for the first time how flat your tummy has gotten. With your hand resting there, it's almost as if you were never pregnant.

Your brother pulls the guest chair closer to the bed, sits with his elbows resting on his knees, looking down at the gray tile floor, and says, "I imagine he's at home. I put him in a cab about seven this morning. His car was still at my apartment when I left."

"Must be nice," you say, and lean back on the pillows, but they feel flat, stiff. Your brother stands and walks to the window, opening the blinds and color comes to the picture. You run your hands through your hair again, feeling as though that incessant crying is going to return. "God, I want a shower," you say.

By the time your parents arrive in the afternoon, you've showered, put on a stiff green gown from your overnight case, French braided your hair, and fed the baby again, this time a bit more successfully. You still haven't had any real sleep and you're cross, even as you greet them—your kisses slight and hugs quick. But you hold your father's hand as you sit propped against the pillows, the sheets fresh, tucked and folded precisely by the nurses. The sheets are rough on your skin—your elbows feel rug-burned. You take the complimentary bottle of lotion from the tray on the bed-table, start rubbing it on your hands, your elbows. Your father takes the bottle, takes over, rubbing the greasy pink into your skin.

Your niece, your sister's child, sits in your mother's lap, her perfect blond curls spread against your mother's burgundy sweater. The child's hand reaches up and toys with your mother's beads while staring at you. She says, "What's wrong with her eyes?" Your mother's arms squeeze around her, an affectionate gesture, and, not quite whispering, she says, "She's been crying. Having a baby hurts and she's been crying." Then your mother kisses her on the cheek and looks at you, smiling still, smug in her correctness. The child stares at you again and you can't imagine why your mother brought her.

"Where's your mommy?" you ask.

She looks up at your mother who is holding the child's hands between her own now, and your mother looks back at her, saying, "Tell her she's at work. Say 'she'll come by when she gets off'."

The child looks down at her hands and says, "At work. She'll come by. . ." and her face turns back to your mother's, questioning. Your mother whispers in her ear and the child finishes, "when she's off." Your mother squeezes her again and they look at each other, there's a quick kiss between them, and then smiles.

You turn your attention to your father. "Have you seen the baby?"

He nods, grinning, screwing the cap back on the lotion, and in a teasing voice, says, "Looks like a baby. They all look the same to me." You laugh and it feels nice between you. He puts the lotion in the tray of the bed-table and you notice the smile fade and then his eyes settle on you somberly.

"Has this happened before, Daddy? In our family? Do you know? It seems to me I remember someone telling me about something like this, years back. . . ."

Your mother laughs, having missed the transition somehow, missed the fact that your father is no longer in a teasing frame of mind, that it's serious. "Of course not," she says, her cheeks, her fat neck blotching red now under your father's stare, rocking back and forth with her arms around the child.

You ignore her and look back at your father. He's shaking his head no, "Not that I know of, darling." And the room is quiet. A baby is crying down the hall. Your father shifts his stance by the bed and says, "This is something genetic, then? Is that what they say?"

You touch the books on the bed beside you. "That's what these say." You haven't had time to look at them much, to read much, but you'd skimmed through them before your parents arrived, reading here and there, and the pictures were so shocking, the grotesque images presented were such that you steer your father's hand away as he reaches for them, saying, "No, Daddy, you don't want to." A baby cries down the hall again and you know it isn't yours. "My baby's not that bad. His case is not that bad." You feel the damn tears skirting your eyelids, hot, and you sit and say, "Daddy, hand me my robe there. Let's walk down to see the baby." He helps you slip into your matching robe and you wiggle your feet into the almost matching slippers. When you stand, tying the robe at your waist, pleased that you have one again so soon, your mother says, "We'll wait here," and she and the child stare at you. You take your father's arm and walk down the hall toward the nursery.

Your sister puts in an appearance, mannered at best. There's nothing between you but years of fighting over crayons, the front seat of the car, the hair dryer, makeup, attention. Nothing warm or affectionate in your relationship. You don't like her very much, her ways, her extremely proper behavior and plastic kisses. She, you know, doesn't approve of you, of your not quite traditional sense of things. So there you are.

When she leaves, you settle back into reading the books. Like a masochist, you soak it up page by page, the horrid pictures, black gaping holes in infant faces, disfiguring scars, children that would have been beautiful, the cross sectioned, numbered processes of surgical repair, thick tubes jutting from the mouths of severe cases, tongues located in throats. You read of the certainty of speech impediments, the likelihood of hearing loss, the possibility of retardation. And you learn that it usually takes more than one surgery to fix it, a cleft like your son's—sometimes three or four. And then later, when puberty comes, and he's outgrown his surgically created mouth, they'll have to build him a new one and his tongue will have to learn to use it again, to speak all over again. But he'll get through that, and you will too. Then he'll pick a beautiful bride from one of the dozens that will fall in love with his eyes and you'll inflict your final pain—because no one will do it but you. You'll sit beside your happy, strong son and show him books like these and he'll turn the pages in horror and you'll tell him, you'll have to tell him—you have a 50-50 chance of passing this to your child.

You close the book in your lap, the pages falling past your fingers, and swipe angrily at the tears, but they won't quit coming. There's nothing in you now to stop them.

Your face is still wet when your husband wakes you, lifting one of the books from your lap. He switches on the lamp beside the bed, settles in the guest chair, and starts flipping through the pages. He's changed his clothes from the night before, but his shirt doesn't match his slacks, and you would have told him not to wear those shoes. In the light of the lamp, you see creases in his face you've never noticed before and his eyes are shadowed, red-rimmed. You're almost ashamed because you can't find it in yourself to pity him. It feels as though you've lived an entire week without him. As he turns the pages of the book, you know he won't see what you saw. He won't bother to read the words. He won't grasp the thing the way you have. He'll live it a day at a time, you think.

He looks up at you from a pictured page and says, "We should thank God—it could have been so much worse."

You frown at him and say, "Thank God? Thank him for what? That he saved the worst for that poor child?" and you point towards the pitiful baby in the picture. He closes the book and leans back in the chair, staring at you, puzzled.

"And what do you suppose that poor baby's parents had to be thankful for?" You're staring him down; you won't budge on this.

He leans toward you, almost whispering, "No one knows why these things happen, but—" You hear your mother in his words.

"Do you know why no one knows? Is it not obvious to you why no one can figure this out?" You're almost shouting now, and your stomach is cramping. "Because it is illogical, absolutely inexcusable!"

Your husband stands and places the book hard on the bed-table. "That—you—that attitude of yours—that's probably why." He's breathing hard, his face reddening, and leaning toward you, his hands firm on the bed, he says in a whisper, "Nature has a way of preventing this. It's called miscarriage, and it's what your body tried to do, if you'll remember, when you were three months pregnant. But your great doctors stepped in and you popped Brethine for the next six months every time you felt the least contraction."

The gray haired nurse comes through the door, wheeling the baby in front of her. You roll your eyes to the ceiling and take a deep breath. Your husband turns away, facing the window, wiping his face with his hand.

"Are we ready to try this again?" asks the nurse.

Your husband walks to the door, a slight glance toward the baby.

"Yes," you say. "Why don't you run along to the chapel now or the bar which seems more likely and, in the meantime, I'll stay here and try to figure out a logical way to feed our baby without drowning him." You don't know if he's heard you, because he's long gone out the door and the nurse, whom you despise, is standing over you, holding your baby, looking over her glasses at you. You hold your arms out for the baby and after she hands him to you, she steps back and says softly, "You know, I'd like to see this little fella go home to a happy, stable environment. He's got troubles enough as it is."

You stare up at her. *Incredulous*, you think, and you say, "Well, you won't be there, so that's one pleasantry we can count on, isn't it." And you can't believe you've said it, you would never have said it, but there—it's done.

As you prop the baby into feeding position, you see her out of the corner of your eye. She sets the bottle on the bed-table and walks out on silent soles, her hosed thighs rubbing. You take the bottle, turn it so the hole faces the baby's tongue, and as he eagerly takes it in his mouth, you say, "There now. It's all done now." You squeeze gently on the bottle and the arms flail out, the head pushes back. You remove the bottle, grab a tissue from the bed-table, and wipe milk from his nose. You hold him to you, the warmth of his head against your cheek, his mouth near your ear, to hear the breath catch. And in that moment, when the tiny gasp sounds, you feel a satisfaction that you've never known. You kiss his cheek, his eyes, his nose, his red milky mouth and prop him on your lap again. You hold the nipple to his mouth and he takes it. Again.

Slivers

She stands near the entrance of Wal-Mart, a row of push mowers flanking her right, tiers of petunias wilting on her left. She faces entering customers, a cardboard placard strapped over her shoulders and hanging to below her knees. The placard is trimmed in florescent orange tape, and, in black print that you can see half the parking lot away, it reads, "I am a shoplifter, caught in the act of stealing from this store. Sentenced by Judge Perkins."

She's maybe fifteen, sixteen and one look tells me that there's a parent somewhere cringing over her predicament, maybe from embarrassment, maybe from helplessness—not being able to protect her from this. The care invested in her is visible—there's a gloss, an aura, a cleanness of presentation—her hair, her skin, her eyes, her nails. I wince as I get closer to her; she's pitiful. Our eyes meet, embarrassment running both ways. I look away, to others. A heavy set woman pants along beside me, toddler on her hip. She seems not to notice the girl. Two boys pass me, the wide bottoms of their jeans scuffing the sidewalk. The tallest, about the same age as this girl, says to the other, "What a genius."

The greeter offers me a shopping cart, says, "Hello. How are you today?" I smile, nod, but it haunts me like a bad wreck, that lovely girl exposed that way. I don't see how that can be good for business. Can't remember now what I had planned to buy. I push the cart to get out of the way of other shoppers, those coming through the door unaffected, shoppers with a purpose. *What if her friends see her? A teacher? A neighbor? Her Sunday School teacher? That age—yeah—this could do it—do her in.*

I push the cart along, following wide paths that lead into the maze of smaller aisles, finding myself near the back of the store in front of a large bin of bed pillows. Didn't come to buy pillows, but put two in the shopping cart. *Who is this Judge Perkins? How could he do that to her?* And big, big notions come to me about America and smiley-face economics and justice and mostly it's all too big for me to make sense of—a confusion of thoughts that leaves me feeling terribly blunt. *It's a shame.* That's the gist of it, I suppose. But as I maneuver the cart around shoppers stalled in aisles, and aisles too packed for easy passage, I'm thinking at base *It's wrong—justice should feel right—it shouldn't be embarrassing to look at.* And then I remember what I came to buy.

Half the aisle on one side is row beside row of Hot Wheels cars. Must be a hundred different models to choose from. You'd think, *grab one; let's go.* Not so easy, though; Devin has a collection of eighty-two and at six years of age he doesn't want duplicates. He wants the models he doesn't have. Certain ones please more than others. Nothing bizarre for Devin. He wants the realistic model— sharp, yes, but realistic. No helicopters or hydroplanes either. He sticks to the road, to city streets and interstates. And no construction vehicles—not today—though he would be perfectly willing to set up detours around road construction work. But Lyle works construction and the last thing I want Devin to think about today is his father.

It's last night, the way Lyle treated Devin last night, the way I let Lyle treat Devin last night, that makes this choice of Hot Wheels cars so important. That's why Devin has so many cars. I want him to forget. Want to counter the bad. Balance the scales. I pick out a fuchsia Cruiser and study its details, wondering how much longer something as small as a Hot Wheels car can do that. I'll pick five new ones today. Can't imagine one being enough.

All day I've been kicking myself—I should have made sure when Devin came in from playing yesterday that he had put his bike away. From now on, I'll have to remember that. There's so much I have to remember for Devin's sake. But last night, the thing was the bike. Lyle had worked overtime, and it was almost Devin's bedtime when he came home. The backdoor slammed and Lyle found us in the den playing Devin's game of Memory. He jerked Devin up by his arm, then leaned down till they were face to face.

"Haven't I told you ten million times not to leave your damn bike in the yard. Where's it go?"

Devin stood speechless, staring at the floor. A hard look is really all it takes to break his heart.

"Answer me; where's it go?"

Devin eyed me.

"Look," I said, "the bike—it's my fault. I called him in from playing to eat. Said, 'leave what you're doing and get in this house right now.' I forgot he was supposed to put his bike up." All this was a lie—a good one I thought.

"Shut up," Lyle said through his teeth, not taking his eyes off Devin. "Quit defending him. He knows better. Don't you, Devin."

Devin kept turning his head to look at me. I shifted to the edge of the couch and froze. And that's a hard, hard thing to do—a thing that grows in hardness every time you have to do it. A thing doubly hard because you know in the back of your mind that you don't have to do it.

"What you looking at your mamma for?" Lyle asked and shook Devin by the shoulders. "And, Jesus, quit your crying." Then grabbing Devin by the back of his shirt, Lyle half pulled, half dragged him through the long hall, through the kitchen, and to the back door. He opened it—pushed Devin out onto the deck. "Now get your ass out there and put that bike in the carport. Next time I find it left out you ain't gonna get a chance to put it up."

It was Devin's worst fear—going outside in the dark—alone—and our yard covers more than an acre, pitch dark at night. His eyes were pleading, his shoulders slumped, hands gripping his pants at the sides. Sympathy was pouring from me to him—I'm sure he could see that—but how far does that take a kid?

"I'll go with him," I said and tried to push past Lyle to get to him.

Lyle slammed the door. "You won't. That's what's wrong with him now. You baby him all the time."

"C'mon, Lyle," I said. "You know he's afraid of the dark. Don't do this to him."

Outside, Devin panicked, screaming and banging on the door. Begging.

"Lyle, please—"

"No! He gets the bike up or he doesn't come in." Lyle hit the door twice from inside and yelled loud and slow, the veins bulging in his neck.

"Get the bike now! What part of that do you not understand?"

Devin stopped screaming. It was quiet.

"There. Why's it so hard for him to do what I ask? Put his damn bike up when he's done riding—that's all I ask him to do."

But I wasn't in the kitchen with Lyle then. Not really. I was with Devin, remembering how it felt to learn what he was learning. He'd be scared at first, yeah I remember that, but there would be a point when the fear would turn to anger. A point when he would get so mad he'd dare something to come out of the dark to get him because he'd want to take it on. He'd want to get his hands in flesh and squeeze out blood. *C'mon*, he'd be thinking, *come and get me now. I'll kill you.*

Lyle was saying, "What the hell *you* crying for? I don't know 'bout you, but when my daddy told me to do something, he only had to tell me once. I'd never forget it after that. 'Cause if I did, he'd wear my ass out. Never had to be reminded. And I respect the hell out of that man."

I don't understand that kind of respect. I don't know from where it is born.

Devin came through the back door and slammed it. The cordless fell from its nook on the wall.

"That any way to shut the door?"

"No, sir," Devin said.

"Get the bike up?" Devin nodded. "Gonna leave it out there again?"

"No, sir," Devin said.

Lyle looked at me—Father of the Year—satisfied.

And so I'd stood by, watching my son's father teach him things I never wanted him to learn.

I held my hand out toward Devin, said, "C'mon. Let's get your bath."

He took my hand and we walked through the house together until we were out of Lyle's sight. Then I went down on my knees, lifted my slender boy, and carried him up the stairs. In the bathroom, I didn't put him down, but stood in front of the mirror, my eyes closed, rocking him back and forth. He wasn't crying. He was limp, his head heavy on my shoulder. I ran his water, helped him undress. He stared at the faucet. We didn't speak. I wondered—how long? How long before he stops taking my after-the-fact hand? How long before he sees me, finally, as the bad guy—the one who could do, but doesn't? And later, I sat for a long time on the edge of his bed, smoothing the hair around his ear, across his forehead, pitying the smallness of his hand.

I had been a year younger than Devin when I learned that mother was the culprit—accomplice, at least, but I judged her the actual culprit—the savior that turned her back to me. What I remember is a small stretch of desolate beach—not the ocean—an inlet maybe, but certainly connected somehow because there was seaweed, and brine, the taste of it, the way it puckered my lips, and the water was full of stinging nettles. *He* told me it was full of stinging nettles. Or maybe it wasn't. Maybe he only said that to make sure I wouldn't go in the water when they told me to stay there in the sand and play—they'd be right back, but I was not to move from that spot. That was right after we had lunch; he'd cooked steaks on the pit.

"Stay right here, got me? If you come up to the cottage, I'll bring you back down and throw you in with the stinging nettles," he said.

Mother had laughed, slapped his arm, and then, hand in hand, they walked back up the steep hill of sand, toward the cottage on the other side. I sat, digging in the sand with my yellow shovel, making holes I'd fill with water that I'd scooped up carefully in my yellow bucket, afraid the stinging nettles would send their tendrils after me. I was alone on this stretch of beach except for one woman from another cottage further down. She looked to be asleep in her lounge chair.

They left me there so that by late afternoon I had worked myself into a frenzy, the lady in the lounge chair sitting up only when my crying turned to wailing. I was quivering with frustration because they wouldn't come for me and I wanted to be in the cool cottage—wanted water from the faucet. I had walked up to the top of the hill, to where I could see the cottage, and that's when the wailing had set in that stirred the lady in the lounge chair. This lady walked over to me, knelt with her knees in the sand and pulled me to her, between her broad thighs, trying to hug me, but her skin was oily and smelly and I stiffened and cried harder, looking at the cottage. They never came to the door. Never moved the curtains at the windows. I pushed hard against the lady and she took her arms away, but tried to hold my hands. I reached up and grabbed her fat cheeks in my fists, squeezing, gritting my teeth, a cat-like growl churning in the back of my throat. She fell backwards in the sand, red marks covering her cheeks, saying, "Ok. It's ok," shocked, frowning, lifting herself up and brushing sand from her arms, her hands. She walked back toward her lounge chair and sat there, only glancing up the hill at me from time to time. And it had felt good to hurt her. It tired me.

I sat on top of the hill then, staring at the cottage, waiting, my arms wrapped around my shins, my head propped on my knees. It was all right then because I hated them. Hated the fat lady in the chair. Hated them in the cottage. And it stayed all right until the first shadows hit the sand, the sun sinking behind the cottage, the mosquitoes swarming. The fat lady had begun collecting her things, folding her lounge chair. And then I wanted her again, her in the cottage. Wanted to crawl into her arms and have her stroke my face with her cool fingers.

The fat lady came to me, her hands full. "That your cottage there?" she asked.

I nodded.

"Want me to walk you back?"

All the way to the cottage, I cried. I believed he was mean enough to bring me back down and throw me in the water, in with the stinging nettles. I believed my mother couldn't stop him if he decided to.

"Go on in now," the lady said. "Want me to wait here to make sure you're okay?"

I shook my head no; didn't want her to hear him yelling at me.

The screen door slapped shut behind me. They were there, mother sprawled across him on the couch, sleeping, a plate of lemon rinds and a liquor bottle on the floor beside them.

As I come out of Wal-Mart, I'm partly aware that there is a kid close on my heels with a shopping cart he can't control, his mother, twenty steps behind, trying to catch up with him. I bear left to get out of his way, but grab the handle of his cart to keep him from rolling it into the side of a passing car. It scares him, me grabbing his cart. He takes his hands off the handle and backs up three steps into his mother. Out of breath, she says, "Thanks," tugs the boy's shirt at the shoulder and he resumes pushing the cart under her guidance.

The girl with the placard is standing almost beside me in the same spot she was in before and my heart sinks. It would be nice to say something to her, I think. But I can't decide on a single thing.

I decide to ditch the wobbly-wheel cart right there—pillows are big, but not heavy. Lifting the bag out of the cart, I realize I'm standing right in front of the girl now and it occurs to me that, standing in this position, holding this huge bag, I'm blocking her sign. And for maybe half a minute I think about standing right there in front of her until she's done paying her dues. Instead, I look at my watch and head toward the car—only fifteen minutes before I'm suppose to pick Devin up at his friend's house. There's a kid out there right now that desperately needs these Hot Wheels cars. Or at least I desperately need for him to have them.

Devin has enough time to play with his new cars before Lyle comes home. I've chosen well and he's all smiles and motor sounds while I cook supper. I make sure he puts them away in his collection case a good thirty minutes before it's time for Lyle to drive up, and I'm thinking I've got this thing under control—tonight will be a good night.

Nights with Lyle used to be good. He was incredible before Devin was born and I loved him with everything I had to give. It was easy because he loved me back the same way. But since that first week after we brought our son home from the hospital, ever since Lyle said in a late night mumble and with much too much anger in his voice, "Let him cry. Can't jump every time he whimpers," ever since I lay there beside him in that bed feeling as though my heart were being torn asunder, ever since then, a hardness has been growing between Lyle and me. And the thing that makes it impossible to soften the hardness is that Lyle thinks he's being a wonderful father. He can see no other way.

Now, the first thing Lyle says to Devin when he walks through the door is "I see you put your bike away when you were done with it today." And five new cars are forgotten.

"Actually, he didn't touch it today," I say and brush past Lyle with plates and silverware for the table.

"Have I got time for a shower?" he asks.

"Nope. Unless you want your supper cold." The correct answer, the one that would've ensured a pleasant night, would've been *We'll wait—no hurry.* But tonight, already, I'm tired of Lyle.

When he comes to the table after washing his face and hands, he's in a mood. I busy myself fixing Devin a plate, remembering not to give him too much of anything, to give him only the slimmest portions, because Lyle despises food left on a plate. I'm nervous for Devin, afraid he'll do something wrong—spill his milk—wipe his hands on his pants—forget to chew with his mouth shut. One night of all well with Devin is all I want.

"You should have seen this girl today at Wal-Mart," I start, just to break the mood around the table. "She was standing out front with this huge sign hanging on her that said, 'I'm a shoplifter.' Some judge named Perkins made her do it."

"Yeah? See—now that's a good judge there. Bet she don't do it anymore."

We eat in silence. Lyle finishes first, then sits, plate pushed back, elbows on table, sipping tea and watching Devin.

"What's wrong with those potatoes, Dev?" he asked.

I look at Devin's plate—he's eating everything except his potatoes. Then it hits me—he hates gravy. Devin looks at me, clearly upset with me this time. *This is your fault*—that's what he's thinking—has to be thinking it.

"Here, Devin, let me get those—I'll eat those. You can have some without gravy," I say.

But Lyle says, "He can eat 'em."

My hand stops in mid-air as I reach for his plate. I turn to Lyle, "He hates gravy. You know he can't stand it. I put it on there. And besides, I want some more." I reach for his plate again.

Lyle raises his voice and says, "He can eat them. He *will* eat them. No sense in a kid being so picky about his food. Good enough for us—good enough for him."

Lyle is leaning into his elbows now, watching Devin. There is nothing left on his plate but the potatoes. Devin tries to get a forkful to his mouth, but as it gets close to his lips, he puts it back down slowly and the tears are working into his eyes already. He knows what is about to come. And that setting down of the fork is what Lyle was waiting for. He's up out of his chair the second the fork touches the plate, standing over the table.

"Eat those potatoes, Devin. Eat them or I'm gonna feed them to you myself."

Devin manages to get a forkful into his mouth, but he's crying, silently, and he can't chew or swallow. He gags as if he's going to be sick. And I've seen this so many times I'm sick, too, but in a different kind of way. I am so tired of Lyle. I cannot watch this. I cannot do this tonight.

"Eat the shit!" Lyle yells, and I jump in my chair.

Devin is crying harder—mutely—and potatoes are beginning to sputter around his lips. He can't get them down and he knows the consequences of spitting them out. Lyle starts around the table.

I'd watched Lyle force peas down Devin once. I know that if this happens tonight, nothing will ever be the same between Devin and me. I push my chair back, directly into Lyle's path. I pull Devin's chair out from the table and cup a napkin in my hand around his mouth. "Get rid of it," I say, and grab another napkin to clean his mouth up with when he's done.

Lyle is ranting, "You better eat those potatoes, boy." He shoves my chair out of his way, tries to shove me out the way. I take Devin's plate and sling it like a Frisbee across the room. It smacks against the wall leaving splatters of potatoes and gravy on the paneling, the carpet beneath. I urge him out of his seat, my hands on his arms, and escort him to the bottom of the stairs. "Run up and start your bath, Devin. I'll be up in a bit." I watch him walk half-way up the stairs.

In the dining room, Lyle is in the same spot, hands on hips, chewing the inside of his cheek. My legs tremble, my hands shake, but I grab two glasses from the table and head for the kitchen. Lyle moves suddenly toward me and I flinch as I pass into the kitchen. He grabs my hair with a jerk that spins me half-around and I stumble against the stove, dropping the glasses. A saucepan of warm bouillon hits the floor.

"Don't ever get between me and my son again," he says, his hand still wrapped in my hair, jerking to emphasize his words. "Do you understand me?" I stare at him and my fear is gone. My head is ringing, *C'mon you son of a bitch. C'mon.* He lets go, squinting his eyes at me and chewing the inside of his cheek again. I back up a few steps till I step on something sharp—the dropped glass. Tiny slivers span the tiled floor. Lyle sees it, too. He looks at his boots. He looks at my bare feet. Then he grabs me to him, arms around my waist.

"You're feeling awful cocky tonight, huh— where you getting all this energy I wonder," he says, swaying me in his arms.

I keep my arms between us, "From you, baby. It's all from you." I drape my arms across his shoulders. "Now, c'mon, you. Let's dance," I say and take a step forward.

His arms tense around me, his face puzzled.

I squeeze his shoulders, forcing a tilt, and say, "I just want to dance. Matter of fact, I'm going to dance you all over this kitchen." I'm playing the lead and he's totally off balance.

He reaches up for my arms, but I yank him back to me hard, so hard he catches hold of my waist. His boots crunch as we move across the floor, and suddenly the floor under me is smeared with blood and when I look down, there is the warm bouillon on the floor, too, mixing with the glass and blood, stinging my feet. He pushes me from the waist, trying to regain control, but I'm holding tight around his shoulders, forcing tilts to the left, to the right, dancing little box-steps, and he's crazy with it. Then I let go and he stands there, stunned.

"Never again," he whispers in my face. "This is nothing—nothing." He backs away from me, looking at the floor, then at me as if I fill him with disgust.

Then I'm alone, standing in the middle of the kitchen, like a tightrope walker. Can't move because it hurts too bad. I lift a foot to take a step, but the weight on my other foot drives the slivers deeper. I stand like this maybe three, four minutes, then pull my shirt over my head, bend slowly, my feet on fire, and swab one spot on the floor near me free of glass and blood. I sit in the cleared spot and take a deep breath, looking at the floor, at my feet.

I think about Devin taking his bath upstairs, the gloss of his skin when he's wet, the pinkness of his nails. Devin clean. Devin free. I think about how the night could have ended.

Lyle clomps through the house, coming back. He stands in the door of the kitchen. "Shit. You're messed up." Then he comes to me, places his hands under my arms to lift me. "Jeez'um, look at this shit."

I grab a sharp chunk beside me, what used to be the bottom of the glass, and flail it about behind me wanting to sink it into him—I don't care what part of him. "Leave me be, Lyle," I holler. "Don't you dare—you don't get to do this." I feel the glass chunk make contact and let it go. There's no sound of it hitting the floor. I bend my head to my knees, dizzy, drop my hand to the floor and trail my fingertips in the mess of blood and bouillon and gritty slivers of glass. "I did this—*me*—this blood is mine."

Substitute

They pulled J.W. straight out of the water onto the pier, pencil thin moccasins tangled around his ankles like Ramen noodles. He'd cannon-balled off the pier's end three times already. Each time he climbed the ladder back up, he'd wink and flick water from his fingers at me. I knew too well he loved me—adored me. When he came near me, people would watch, smile. I'd been ignoring him contentedly, lazily, eyes closed against the glare of sun on lake, stretched on a thick yellow towel near the landing of the pier. He was here. I was here. We would be in the water together soon enough, as soon as the adults gave up the heat for the comfort of air conditioning. His shadow crossed me and water pelted my legs and stomach as he shook his head over me.

"J.W., quit," I said, the water too cold because the sun was too hot.

"Swim with me," he said. "Come on—get wet—cool off."

"Go," I said and slid an oiled foot up and down his cool shin, then rested my hot toes on his cold ones. "In a minute," I added because I thought then there would be a minute—an hour, days, nights, decades—that he would be there when the others went inside, when I was ready to brave the shock of cold lake. And so I took my time, his in hindsight, ours, took it for a given.

It was some great coincidence that we'd both been raised in a place called Brink, born in the same hospital, same day, same recorded hour and minute, bringing our fathers together to stare through the nursery window, to laugh over the coincidence of time, later to fish the lake, then other lakes and two-family camping trips.

We kissed tight lipped when we were eight and dared each other out of our bathing suits under the water, giggling. We touched and wrestled when we were twelve, under the pier, naked, in awe of our bodies—the way our bodies allowed us to feel—trying to make sense of what to do with them to help the ache, straining to be as close as we could be. By sixteen, we had grown to know our bodies well. His was made for baseball, for swimming, for running, for dancing, for tanning in the sun, for my hands. Never did we question that—the fact that his body was made for my hands. There was no competition. We were too busy with each other to notice anyone else. His "swim with me" was always an erotic invitation—to join him in the water, to allow his fingers to slip across my nipples and into the tiny bottoms of my bathing suit, to explore to the point of aching.

I would join him eventually—I was only teasing. It worked, the teasing, because he knew it and I knew it for what it really was. This was the way we spent our days. It was all foreplay—we were forever in a frenzy. The sun would heat, the lake would cool, we ached and ached and ached. An endless, luxurious cycle.

This time, I watched J.W. sprint across the slimy planks, the way he took to air freeze-framed, a posing muscle-man, one wild whoop and into the water feet first. I thrilled to think of letting him slip my bottoms down in the water, me holding to the ladder of the pier, letting him touch me as he pleased, his cock pressing naked against my belly maybe, or my thigh. Mostly he'd come with his fingers snug inside me and mine gripping his cock. And thinking this, I smiled and sensed a gentle throb and closed my eyes again: no hurry.

No one looked when he burst to the surface, screeching; he was always screeching, or whooping, or hollering. Not immature for sixteen; just very alive. I smiled with my eyes closed. But when he said, "Jesus Christ," everyone stiffened. And soon two men were reaching out to his clawing hands. They heaved him up onto the pier, but yanked free from his grip and back-stepped six, seven feet away, the snakes fast slithering in erratic paths to return to the water, hanging over the edge of the pier like crooked daisy stems, then plopping into the lake, little snake head dots rippling the surface.

J.W.'s mother, Ivey, started and fell off her lounge chair in the sand beside the pier. But when she got to her feet, sand clinging to the oil on her arms and legs, she froze, hunched over like a shortstop, eyes wide, like the ball was coming straight at her and she couldn't get her glove up.

The men on the pier were snapping heavy beach towels at the few moccasins that took shelter between J.W.'s legs. J.W. lay prone, his whole body jerking like a marionette in the hands of a two-year-old, his feet and ankles already swelling, peppered with red-black holes, lips tinged, like he'd been in the water too long. The snakes were coiling back from the dull whips of the towels, then latching onto J.W.'s trembling thighs. He would tilt his head back sharp, breath held, one beat, two, the body wondrously still, controlled, then released, the air seething out through the teeth, flecks of foam on his lips, the marionette dancing wildly again.

One of the women ran for a cellular in her car. I grabbed the plastic paddle out of the inflatable, ran past the men, and one by one, spatula-flipped the three little snakes off the pier. I settled beside J.W.'s shaking body. I looked at his long, thin legs, legs beginning to look like a man's, the fuzzy curls I loved to fingertip now slick straight and dark against his skin, looked at his swelling ankles, his feet, and I knew—you don't fix this. The swelling was so rapid, it seemed the skin would give into splits. And the men, calling for wives to find belts, took the too-thick beach towels and tried to tourniquet his legs. I looked at first one man, then the other, but they wouldn't look back. I put my hands on each side of J.W.'s face because he couldn't hold still, but it was as if his mouth was swelling inside, or maybe his tongue, and he was struggling with it and jerked his head about.

Ivey's nails scratched into my shoulder as she pulled me away. She took my place, and kissed his forehead—*just little snakes, J.W., just babies, you're all right, I've got you J.W.* Sand was sprinkling off her arms onto his chest and she busied herself wiping it off of him, every sweep of her hand causing more to shake loose onto him, until she began to weep from the futility of it all.

He seemed to empty of everything at once. Forcefully. His stomach gave forth. His bowels. The men turned him, so he wouldn't choke on the vomit, but his lungs wouldn't draw air. Then, he lay quiet on his side, the marionette tossed away. His eyes came open and settled a gaze across the water. He saw it. I watched him see it. We all watched him see it. There was a moment when the seeing of it stopped. You could have drawn a line across that moment. It was that clear. That obvious. Only Ivey missed it, busy wiping spittle—one long gleaming thread of spittle from J.W.'s lips, caught like liquid crystal in the sun, something of it still alive.

"They're going to get a foster child," mother had said, her hair twisted round into a knot at the back of her head, held in place by a mere pencil.

I touched the point of the pencil and asked, "For what?"

Mother looked up from her pottery wheel, perplexed, her eyes a dull brown, "What do you mean, 'for what?'" And we stared at one another briefly, not understanding the other's confusion. She looked as if it was supposed to make perfect sense—self-explanatory. She couldn't understand why I didn't immediately grasp the obvious. She brought her arm up to rub her nose, the gray-white ooze of the clay trailing down her wrists.

"They can't replace J.W.," I said, and heard the uneasiness of my own agitation.

She stood then and grabbed a stained towel from the workbench. "That's not what they're doing," she said.

"They would do this if J.W. were still alive?" I asked, leaning to catch her attention.

"No," she said, refusing to look at me, only rubbing her hands over and over in the towel.

I nodded, "They're trying to replace J.W."

She sat back on her pottery stool and sighed toward me. "Maybe a little," she said, then straightening, added, "Ivey needs this."

"Ivey needs this," I said, digesting the obvious.

Mother stared at me a minute longer, then flipped the switch for the pottery wheel. It started its familiar hum-rattle noise. I walked around behind her as she dipped her fingers in her water bowl, leaned over, putting my arms around her shoulders, my cheek against hers. She was about to put her fingers to her work when I asked, "You would need this if I were gone?"

She flipped the switch to "off," sighed again, and said, "Darling, I cannot imagine what I'd need." She turned on her stool to look at me. "Please try to understand. It would help Ivey so much if you understood."

J.W. had died on May twenty-third. Ivey brought her foster *child*, Chris, into our world on August fifth. Up until that day, I'd suffered sunburn after sunburn, laying on my side on the pier, looking out across the lake, trying to see it the way J.W. saw it last. I decided that it wasn't really the lake he saw, and I would lay there, hours, trying to slow everything down, my heart, my breathing, tried to make everything stop for just a second or two, knowing if I laid there long enough, emptied myself thoroughly enough, it would come to me. I snitched Valium from Ivey, trying to induce something—whatever it was—the thing in J.W.'s eyes just before the seeing stopped. I thought I would know it when I saw it—I was sure I would know it. With the Valium, I fell asleep on the pier. For days I suffered that burn, the blisters, the peeling.

I visited Ivey every day before Chris came. She never mentioned it to me, the fact that she had applied for a foster child. We worked on refinishing her dining room table and chairs, leisurely. Ivey didn't have the drive to do more than a little at the time. Strip a chair—that's enough for one day, she'd say and stretch her long length toward the ceiling, giving in to a slump. She'd aged so much since JW had died. Her hair had always been a rare white, ever since I was a small child, but now her skin presented the strain, the evidence of destruction. And her dark, dark eyes that used to mirror the light and energy of contentedness were now dull behind heavy lids. She'd grow quiet during my visits and—as though she had forgotten I had come—she'd leave me to go and sit on the balcony where we used to see her doing yoga every evening, staring off at the lake, and she wouldn't have known one way or the other if I'd stayed or left. Most times, I'd leave.

When we'd applied the first touch of stain to bare wood, we delighted in the red-gold hue, the way the sun livened it, and her hand caught my arm in pleasure, saying, "Just what do you think about that. God, but it's lovely." We smiled and clutched hands, staring at the lush blend of colors caught in the grain of the wood. But in one single moment, we checked ourselves. We'd looked at each other, and felt the same thing: a sort of "oops" in the heart—we'd stumbled somehow into a world void of J.W. and happy. It was a raw moment, but something of the warmth lingered and Ivey said, "Things are so much nicer when you're here. Thank you for coming so often to see me." And I thought, how odd, because it seemed that all my life I'd been at her house as much as my own.

He was a year younger than J.W.—than J.W. *was*—than I was. But you could tell he'd lived longer than the both of us put together.

"I'm going out on the pier," I said, when they brought him in, when they'd introduced him and he'd seemed quiet; after I'd noticed the blond hair curling along the point of his chin; after I'd decided you could probably count the hairs there; before I'd determined whether or not he was trying to grow them there or just didn't like to shave. Mother looked perturbed. Ivey looked apologetic. But he, Chris, looked numb. Tired. Everything the opposite of J.W. And I liked him— the tragedy of him—his lackluster eyes, the triangle of three dots tattooed next to his thumb, the mess of hair, sun bleached, partially dreadlocked, the wrinkly button up shirt that hung on his lean frame.

He never looked up when I turned to leave and so I smiled. I walked the narrow pier, black planks stretched tight over the sleeping water of the lake, the No Wake of night. I walked toward the twin lanterns on poles that marked the end, sending white sheets of light floating, arcing toward boats lined up on the opposite shore. It had been an odd occurrence, my father had said, the bevy of moccasins in the lake. They would normally have been in the marsh fields, in the river, but not the lake. Plenty of water snakes in the lake, he said. But not moccasins. None of them poisonous, except the moccasins. The rains washed them in the night before—it must have been. Some little flash flood, sweeping them up in a tangle to catch along the piling of the pier. Perhaps. And so many! he'd said. Not likely to be so many. Seven would be believable. Certainly no more than twelve. Must've been a couple of beds of them, swept up together. And the size of this lake—what are the chances? he'd said.

I lay on my side and stared at the dark lake, shallowed my breathing, closed my eyes, waited, waited, then opened them. Nothing. Black water, lantern light. It wasn't the same at night anyway. I heard Mother talking loudly and turned toward the house. Ivey and Chris were beginning the walk to his new house, foster father trailing a little behind, and I watched them move, taking their time, until Ivey spotted me, and waved, her arm high in the air. It was a happy, happy wave and I waved back and shouted, "Goodnight." Still he did not look my way—this new person in Ivey's life—in our lives. But he did look at her—looked and spoke—and there was a grin, maybe, I couldn't really tell, but there might have been a grin as he looked at her, standing about the same height, his head tilted just so to speak to her with soft words, as if he knew, clearly, the way sound intensifies over the water at night.

I stood between the lantern poles, stared into the far reaches of the lake, and said, "It's a good thing for her, J.W." I heard Ivey's front door close, turned as the lights went on upstairs. It was a beginning again for them, a glitch in the history book. They are turning the page.

I peeled my t-shirt free over my head, a wisp of cool night air settling on me. My jeans clung to my sweaty skin, stubborn against my first tugs. I hadn't been in the lake all summer; I would swim once before summer's end. I stretched my arms from lantern to lantern, moths crisscrossing, circling, daring to touch me with their wings. *This is me, J.W., me.* I curled my toes over the slippery edge and dove into the mirrored light, the cool water rushing, wrapping, swirling around, under, and over. And that sweet lake held me as I bobbed for air, the heat tapering away from my body like steam, the gentle water pulsing, rocking, slapping at the dock in response to me, echoing me as my feet found mud. I stood with arms stretched, ran my fingers over the ripples, returning each long caress, feeling the rhythm of the lake lapping across my breasts, the weight of its body, one drinking kiss, and I knew, for me, there would not be that end.

Cicada

Midpoint of the drag strip, I curl my fingers into the chain link fence, shoulder high, rest my chin on the cool top bar and watch the paired set-go lights. *Yellow—yellow—yellow—green.* The car on the far lane hooks the track on the green, the front end rising strong on the driver's side. You can hear it, the Lincoln transmission, can visualize the driver doing his reach-snatch—one, two, three, four, five levers—so quick. The competitor's car starts clean, no visible hook, but manages zero to one thirty in four point eight seconds with an automatic transmission. A clear win. A disgusting kind of win—no real skill, no real effort, no clutching or snatching with precision, no passionate rise of the front end. The numbers on the board say it's a winner, but it's the car with the Lincoln transmission that moves me. A car worth remembering, a driver that can be proud.

These are things my son taught me to care about. Saturday nights he taught me to feel the thrill of the drag strip. "The trick," he said, "is to not blink when the lights go green. Let the visual come at you with the sound of the engines as the cars move toward and past you—the combination of the two will send you." It's a five second event; a five second thrill.

The next two cars smoke their tires and move into position, waiting on the lights. What kind of car is that, I'm wondering, on the far side? I should know this. I do know this. He told me before. What was it he said? I can almost hear him saying it. What kind for God's sake? This was one of his favorites—a local favorite—Tater Bug. Yes, I remember that, but what kind? A Nova. Looks sort of like an old Nova. No, can't be; why can't I remember? He told me over and over, "Watch this car, that *something* there—Tater Bug—got more heart than any car out here." He's only been gone two weeks—fifteen days ago he stood right here beside me and talked about Tater Bug. I'm forgetting his words. God what else will I forget. Surely not his voice. I couldn't bear to lose his voice. I pat my eyes dry—the lights run the column—Tater Bug hooks, loses, and wins me forever.

My legs are trembling and a man is staring at me from a little way down the spectator's fence. I see him in my peripheral vision. I must look like an idiot—standing out here watching the races, blubbering like a baby. My fingers tighten on the fence and I want to scream at him, "Will you please quit staring at me—I got a right to this—I got a reason for this. My son is dead, damn you. Damn all of you." But instead, I turn to my car behind me. I'd come early so I could park along the fence. The back seat is full—two suitcases of my stuff. The rest was my son's. I couldn't leave it. None of it. Not even his clothes. Especially not his clothes. In the seat beside me are boxes of his model cars. I will find a place. I will build a special shelf for his cars. When I look at them, touch my fingertips to them, I can see him so clearly, hunched over newspaper spread on the dining room table, gluing, painting. "What you thinking about?" I would ask. And he'd cock his head toward me, serious always, and say, "I do this so I don't have to think. You know?"

I did know. There was too much for him, for me, to *not* think about. We were not a perfect family. I open one of the boxes next to me. A yellow '69 mustang. One of the pinstripe decals is starting to peel away. I'll fix it. When I get settled, I'll go through his cars and fix everything. This is the one he cussed over. Couldn't get the struts to set just right. This is the one he was working on when he said "Mom, you're a cicada."

"A what?"

"A cicada," he said, "You know—a dry fly—one of those bugs that comes out of those shell things you find on the side of a tree. Big ugly green bug. The one that makes all the racket in the summer time."

"I know what you're talking about. Thanks heaps. You, son, are a worm."

"You're not big or ugly."

"What then? I make all kinds of racket? What?" I was sitting in the chair across from him working on a crossword puzzle in the local paper.

He put his model down and stared at me. I put my pen down, waiting.

"I was watching this thing on TV about them. They're pretty cool. The female drills little holes in the twigs of a tree. Puts her eggs in them. The twigs die, fall to the ground, and the larvae dig down to the roots of the tree and feed on the sap—get this, this is the cool part—for seventeen years."

I could see where he was going with it now and I didn't like it. I opened my mouth to protest, but he cut me off.

"The seventeenth summer these things start digging their way back out of the ground. They start climbing up the side of the tree till their shell hardens on them and they can't go any further. Then, they bust out of their shell like the Incredible Hulk and fly away free."

He's smiling at me—thinks he's got me pegged.

"So what's your point, son?"

"You've been feeding on sap for years and now you're stuck in a shell on the side of that tree.

You're gonna have to break out of that shell. Ain't normal not to break out."

"I like my shell. My shell is comfortable. I'm perfectly content in my shell."

"You are not. You hate it. You're not happy."

I stood then and said, "I am happy when you and my tree are getting along. Like these days. You guys are getting along fine. Besides, the entire thing is a false analogy. I am not a cicada. I saw that same show the other night. And if I was, think of this—they only live a matter of weeks after they come out of that shell. And when they come out, all they do is mate, lay eggs, and die. The females anyway. The males sit around and sing their horrible songs. The females don't sing at all."

"Why are you so scared to leave him?" Dean asked.

"Leaving is easy Dean. Piece of cake. It's staying that's hard."

My tree is Hogue—but no, not my tree—my husband. I am not a cicada. I had left him before. Three times. The first when he left bruises on Dean. Dean was only eight then. I left him and took Dean to my mother's for a month. Hogue convinced her first, then me, that he would never lay a hand on Dean again. He didn't. He changed. Five years later, when Dean was thirteen, he started leaving bruises on me. I left after the fourth bout. Stayed in a safe house for a week with Dean. The rule was tell no one where the house was, ever, and no contact with anyone for seven days. I called Hogue on day seven. We talked. I took a grumbling Dean home that afternoon. Hogue changed. Never laid a hand on me again in violence. The third time, last year, when I found out Hogue was having an affair, I left again. Stayed in a motel for fifteen days, charging all my expenses to his credit card. I didn't call him. Dean stayed with a friend. He was seventeen then. Hogue found me when he got the credit card bill. Came to the hotel room. He'd lost at least thirty pounds. Looked like hell. I went home. He changed. For years, Hogue's been changing. The pattern is established. Hogue screws up. I leave Hogue. Hogue realizes he's screwed up. I forgive Hogue. Hogue changes. The thing defies all statistics. And each time I left and came back, Hogue mourned the passing of another chunk of his manhood. He would be subdued for weeks. But he and Dean could never get along more than a few days at a time.

"You got a brain," Hogue would yell. "Why you want to piss it away? See these hands? You like the way they look?" Hogue would hold up his hands, forever scarred, the small finger of the left hand missing, fresh welding burns on them. "You want hands like this?"

Dean would roll his eyes.

"Yeah, you do. I can tell. You ain't gonna make it, son. See, you got brains, but you don't use them. You're gonna end up out there with me. And you ain't gonna make it out there either. 'Cause you got no common sense. You ain't gonna make it, son."

Of course, the way Hogue said this, with a kind of "watch and see what I tell you" gleam in his eyes is what made these speeches of his seem something other than fatherly advice. Hogue always had the best intentions. What he wanted for Dean, for me, for us was never far from what I wanted for us. How could I say to Hogue—look, you have the right target in sight, but you're never going to hit it that way—how to say that when he so strongly believed the same thing about me?

I'd go to Dean later, after Hogue's biting speeches. I'd tell him, "Prove him wrong. If I were you, I'd spend the rest of my life trying to prove him wrong."

"I just don't listen to him anymore," he'd say. "You know, in one ear and out the other. Fuck him."

"Just make a mental list. All the things you hate about him—you hate it when he drinks, you hate it when he loses his temper . . ."

"Mom, I said I can handle it. He's fucked in the head. Enough said."

I pleaded with Hogue to keep Dean off the steel till he knew the ropes. "Don't let him up there, Hogue. He's bound and determined he can do anything you can do. I can't stand the thought of him up on the steel. Not yet. Christ's sake, he's only eighteen. What does he know about walking steel?"

Hogue put his arms around me. "I'll keep him on the ground. But the guys will give him hell. He can always coon across on his butt."

"He'd never coon a beam. You know that. If he gets up there, he'll do it like everybody else. You can't let him up is all."

Every night they came home, drinking, Dean proud of his welding burns, the newest cuts on his hands.

"What did you do today?" I asked.

"Don't worry. I played in the sandbox," he would say, and wink at Hogue.

I roll the windows down in the car, lean my head back on the headrest, and listen to the scream of engines. I want to let in the sound, the deafening sound of the engines. I don't want to think. When I think, I get awful pictures in my head. Dean screaming. Dean slipping, trying to hold. Falling.

Hogue explained, three days after the funeral. Hogue couldn't talk till then. Till the third day—the resurrection of Hogue's voice—how I wished it was Dean's. "He was hooking on," he said, "trying to latch his safety harness. He got pissed off at it for some reason. I don't know why. I just heard him raising hell about it. I was walking out to him. . ."

"You told me, promised me, you'd keep him on the ground."

A hand settles on my cheek. I jump. Hogue is there. He walks around the car, opens the passenger door. He starts moving boxes from the front seat to the back.

"Christ, stop it! They're Dean's models. Stop it." I'm bringing the boxes back up to the front. I'm shaking all over.

Hogue leans on the roof of the car, his head hanging, staring down at the ground. He shuts the passenger door gently, comes back around to my side of the car, and opens my door. He puts a knee on the ground, and puts his head in my lap. He is heaving long muffled cries. I put my hands on the steering wheel. He reaches in and wraps one arm around my legs, his hand squeezing into my thigh. I stare out as two cars swoosh past on the track. My hand falls to his head. I don't want it to. I don't want to stroke his hair. Don't want to run my hand across his shoulders. But there's nothing else I can do. His hurt is equal to mine; we had so wanted the same thing. This is the man that made me strong—all those years of practice with this man—learning how to hold without ever really touching, how to look without ever really seeing, to listen without hearing, to smile and kiss and fuck and never feel a thing. I know nothing will ever be harder than this—touching this man, right now. I squeeze the back of his neck, say, "What kind of car is that? Look, look—quick." Tater Bug flashes past, taking a buy back run. He loses.

"That's a Nova," Hogue says, and settles his head back in my lap.

"I was right. I didn't forget. A Nova," I say and smile down at Hogue's dark head.

Crossings

The light from her window forms a long rectangle on the ground in front of me. I can make out the outline of one of the azaleas that grows off to the right, but there are four of the bushes there and big oaks that grow at least twelve feet away from the house on the opposite side, whose limbs hang over it and shade it. Trees too big for climbing, too old to be pretty anymore. I look for them, but they aren't there. No moon or stars tonight, no sky, just black all around, full of things that I know are there. I didn't need light to get through the cornfield though. It's routine now; counting from the back side of the field, I can slip in between the tenth and eleventh row and follow it straight out to her yard. Forty feet more, and there's her window. Maybe even less than that, but it always feels like forty. You can't get off track coming through the cornfield at night, as long as you pick the right row. Once you're in that row, the corn stalks keep you on the same path. When the corn grows tall like it is now, nobody can see you walking across the field.

She's drinking slow tonight. It's Friday and she always takes home a bottle of wine on Fridays. I noticed that before the corn broke the ground. I'd see her across the field, getting out of her car, holding a brown bag twisted skinny at the top. That was before I got up the nerve to walk across at night. Now my toes are numb, pinched in the points of my boots. Two-twenty for these boots. Good leather always pinches at first. I'd give another hundred dollars to be able to whack the back of my heels on the ground a few times, bring some room and feeling back to my toes, but I'm too damn scared to move. Can never wait to get over here, but I know every time it's going to be like this; standing here, too scared to knock my heels, two or three hours some nights, some just twenty, thirty minutes or so. One step forward and all hell would break loose.

One step back and I wouldn't be able to see over the bed, over to where she's sitting in the beanbag chair, down low to the floor, next to the stereo. The bed isn't made, I've never seen it made, and the covers are puffed up, thrown every which way, a blue plaid sheet twisted in a knot on top of the others so it makes it harder to see over the bed. And, too, there's this ugly potter's clay lamp that sits on a nightstand on the window side of the bed and throws shadows all over the place.

I hate that lamp. I see it off to the side, in the corner of my eye, bright as a bare bulb, and I swear, when I close my eyes to sleep at night I can still see it. I wish she would move it to the other side of the bed. Then the shadows wouldn't fall on her so heavy and it wouldn't be glaring there in my eye.

I guess it doesn't matter that she never makes her bed. Nobody there but her and she never has company. I don't make mine in the trailer either, but I think when I get in the new house, I'll make the bed. Probably. Those sheets ought to be on a man's bed. You'd think she'd have pink flowered ones or yellow ones with lace trim. Blue plaid—I don't know. She'll change them now and then, about once a week, but then she puts on plain beige ones.

I wish she'd put that magazine down; *Life*, with a jaguar or leopard or whatever on the cover. How long does it take to look at thirty, forty pictures? At least she's not writing stuff tonight. Sometimes she writes in this red notebook. I can't figure what she writes. Hell, it could be anything—a letter, grocery list, poem, but I think it's a diary or a journal. In the back of my mind there's a plan coming together for finding out what's in that notebook. She keeps it in the magazine rack between the stereo and that brown beanbag chair she sits in. Beige really, but darker than the beige sheets she puts on the bed and it's wide-wale corduroy. She runs her fingers in the grooves of the corduroy when she gets sleepy, when she's about done with her wine sometimes. Out of the dark, a moth flutters in front of my face. I flinch backwards as if someone has thrown something at me and slap at it, curse it quietly. It dips away into the light of the window and flaps about the glass, sweeping it in round passes, until it catches a hold on the casing.

She puts the magazine on the floor beside her, not in the rack, and grabs the wine, wrapping her long fingers around the neck of the bottle. As she turns it up to take a drink, it comes out of the shadows and the wine sparkles red in the light. "There you go," I whisper. She brings the bottle down and holds it to the front of her and the color is lost in the burgundy of her t-shirt. I can only see part of her over the bed and now she slips down in the chair, down in the shadows. But I can hear her humming like it's coming from under water and a dull thumping sound and I know she's tapping her heels up and down, first one, then the other. I can't see her feet. The sounds work their way through the old sideboards of the house and I'm listening so intensely and it's like I can feel it; the dull, beating sounds.

Something, an acorn maybe, falls on the tin roof and clatters along till it falls over the edge with a thump to the ground. She doesn't flinch from the noise like me. Now all I feel is my heart beating. It's in my temples, doing whoosh-whoosh in my ears. And I'm thinking this is freaking stupid. This is just a wee bit sick. What the hell do I do this for? I take a step back with my left foot. I wonder if I'll ever feel my toes again. Now, back with my right and I'm ready to head to the cornfield, but when I look at her again she's standing up, walking back and forth in front of the stereo and chair, the coiled cable of the headphones stretching and relaxing like a slinky. When she turns just so, the light catches in her hair and picks up the different hues of brown and it looks like a deep, rich wood. It's cut short and smooth and it curves under at the bottom so it just touches her earlobes. She looks good when she moves. Something real sensual about the way she moves on those long legs. She's wearing this worn out t-shirt and jeans and a thin gold bracelet, no rings, nothing spectacular, and she's beautiful. Not perfect, not that. Hell, her lips are too big, her tits aren't big enough, her neck is too long—she's got faults. But something makes her beautiful. I can't name it, but I can see it, and when she starts letting go like this, I'm certain of it.

She's drinking faster now, holding the bottle in one hand and playing with the coiled cable with the other. She turns completely around in one spot and the cable wraps her waist and she smiles, her lips wet and berry colored from the wine. I smile too and she starts singing. I can hear it better than I could the humming, can make out a few words, and she's way off key and hitting flats for sharps and if it was anyone else I'd be laughing. There's feeling in it for her though, and I'm studying her face and the emotions there and I'm reading pain. A wind blows up and tosses my hair so I feel visible, like I'm waving a flag for attention. The cornfield livens up behind me in the breeze like a dozen people turning newspaper pages at once and it drowns out the singing. A few hours ago, I was at a barbecue with a hundred other people and I had a woman at my heels, a sure thing for the night, as pretty as they come. What do I do? I sneak away from it all and for what?

She's moving side to side now, a slow dance for one, and I smile and whisper, "For that."

Now she finishes the wine and holds the bottle in front of her and rubs her fingers over the pale, green glass, making paths through the condensation, tracing the label. She turns and drops it in the beanbag chair, pulls the headphones off and sets them on the speaker. She reaches toward the stereo and the red, blinking lights go black. She faces the bed, faces me. Her cheeks are flushed and her eyes say she's more drunk than not. She stares at the bed and runs her thin fingers through her hair, losing them in the brown, and brings them back out to do it again, three, four, five times, all the while still staring at the bed. She walks toward it, toward me, and lies down, slowly. Curling onto her side, facing the lamp, she hugs the balled-up covers to her chest.

Tears break over the bridge of her nose and she pulls the covers in. Her eyes are closed, but the tears still come. One foot rubs against the other, again and again, like a kitten pawing as it nurses. I stick my hands in the pockets of my jeans, push my elbows straight, and watch until her feet are still.

I take my time going back through the cornfield. I never know how to feel afterwards. It isn't a sexual thing; I mean I don't get a hard on watching her. But I know when I close my eyes to sleep tonight I'll get a picture of her in my head, like some freeze-frame, a certain look on her face, some sensual second, and it'll be about sex then. But that doesn't make it perverted—the watching. It would be pretty damn hard to explain if I ever get caught, but the way that house is sitting, like on an island in the middle of cornfields, chances of that happening are slim. If the mailbox wasn't out there by the road, you wouldn't even know there was a house there.

As I walk down the long row, I think back to the first time I saw her. I was driving through a foot and a half of fresh snow, moving back home after the divorce, and she was standing out front of the old Smith house, working on a snow sculpture. It was more elaborate than a snowman. It could have been a replica of Queen Elizabeth or Cinderella or maybe Bette Davis doing Shakespeare. She was in the process of painting it, with what I had no idea, but the lips were scarlet, and the cheeks blushed, and the dress was pale blue. I nearly ran in the ditch that day trying to look back to see it.

I had just bought the land adjoining the Smith place, but I had no idea I'd have a neighbor. The place had been abandoned since I was a kid. The fields were sharecropped every year by the Allens and a share went into an estate account at First Federal Bank in town. I figured she must be some relative of the Smiths. But after I was home a week, it was apparent nobody knew anything about her, except that she worked at Pair's little cinder-block store, and folks called her Sam. Pair didn't know anything about her, just said she did a good enough job for him and that was all he cared. Hell, the mailman didn't even know anything. Said she must have had a P.O. box in town cause she never got mail out here.

Now, I'm thinking, maybe that's part of why I do it. Maybe it's because she's such a mystery. But then, when I lived in the city, in Pittsburgh, there were women all over the place that were mysteries. I worked with women in my office there, beautiful women, that I knew nothing about. What they liked to drink, and what kind of music they listened to, and that was it. And I never thought anything of it. In a place like this though, where everyone knows everyone else, it'll drive you crazy; someone coming here from who knows where and won't reveal anything about herself, so withdrawn from everyone that nobody even feels comfortable enough to ask.

Headlights light up the tops of the corn now and I can hear a motor slowing. I'm a little more than halfway in the field and I hear the downshift and see the headlights swing over the corn, over my head, and I run as fast as I can because someone is turning into my driveway. This is going to look real cute, me coming out of the cornfield in the middle of the night. Jesus Christ, what the hell am I doing? They'll see the jeep, know I'm home. It sounds like Lorn's truck. What the hell does he want now? I hear the truck door close. He's not alone. Nearing the opening of the row, I hear Lorn's voice. There's laughter—how many people did he bring with him? I slow down to catch my breath and step out of the field as quietly as I can. Three shadows are walking toward the lights of the trailer. I sneak over to my jeep. It's parked about ten feet from the truck and just as Lorn reaches up to knock on the door, I flip on the headlights and blow the horn. They all jump, and I get out of the jeep, laughing, and bend over at the waist like it's hysterical. Then I straighten up and say, "Sorry. I've just always wanted to do that. I wish I had it on film." And then I laugh again, like I just can't control it and all the while I'm thinking how damn clever I am.

"How the hell did you get over there without me seeing you?" says Lorn. Lorn is tall and skinny with whitish-blond hair and blue eyes, the kind of eyes that women like to stare at.

"I have my ways," I say, realizing I don't necessarily have to explain anything. I walk toward them and try to figure out who the other two are. One is Steve, but who—oh no they didn't—well hell yeah they did. It's Deborah, the woman that it took me two hours to ditch at the barbecue. I had gone there with Lorn and Steve and they introduced me to her. She's somebody's ex-wife, can't remember whose. She took it upon herself to be my date for the evening, so I took it upon myself to leave at the first chance, only I didn't figure the first chance to be so hard to come by.

Now I guess they want to hang out a while, keep the party going. I'm trying to see if maybe Deborah has latched onto either Lorn or Steve in my absence, but she's walking out to meet me with a sexy grin and she takes my arm and pulls me along to the trailer. Her fingers are warm and she looks at me and says, "Miss me?" The rum is strong on her breath and, as much as I miss doing it, there's no way I'm going to fuck her.

"Lorn, Steve, how come you ain't home with your old ladies?" I ask, and step around a mound of dirt the size of a bowling ball. Deborah's foot catches it and she stumbles, pulling my arm, and giggles.

"Hell, Jim, cause they ain't half as pretty as you," says Steve.

"And Deborah was about to wet her pants to find you," says Lorn, working a toothpick through his teeth.

Everyone is laughing now, but me. I haven't heard anything funny yet. "Well, go on in. It isn't locked," I say because we're standing at the door to the trailer now.

There is no room to move once we're inside. There are two chairs and a stool and four of us, so I stand. I offer beer that hasn't been in the refrigerator long enough to be very cold. They accept and don't seem to notice.

"When do I get to see this house you're building? It's all Lorn and Steve talk about," says Deborah.

I don't want her anywhere near my house, which is only two hundred feet from the trailer. I shrug my shoulders and Steve and Lorn look at each other like they've just figured something out. I open a cabinet above the miniature sink and pull out a flashlight. Deborah looks excited like I'm going to take her over to see the house. I smile at her, then look at Lorn and nod my head toward the door. "Come on Lorn, there's something I want you to check out in the kennels," I say.

Lorn gets up with his beer and Steve starts up too, but I say, "Keep Deborah company, will you?"

"We can all go," says Deborah, standing.

"Sit, Deborah. Sit, girl. I'll bring him back to you," says Lorn. Lorn has always been able to read me pretty well.

The kennels are behind the house and neither is complete yet. But it won't be long and I'll be raising Rottweilers and training them. I've already been assured of contracts with the state police and two security companies. And I know it'll be a cinch to lock in on the doctors and lawyers and anyone who wants it to look as though they have as much money as the doctors and lawyers.

We follow the beam of the flashlight down the hill. We stop at the fence, ten feet high, cost practically as much to put in the fence line as it did to build the damn kennels. I lift the padlock, it's just hanging on the catch, and swing the gate open.

"Nice boots," Lorn says.

I shine the light on them. "Yeah, but they're killing my feet. Hadn't quite got them broke in yet."

We stop right outside the kennels and take two empty ten gallon buckets, flip them upside down, and sit on them.

"So what's up?" says Lorn.

I turn the flashlight out and think about what I want to say. It's more comfortable in the dark.

"I don't want her here."

"Deborah? Come on, Jim, she ain't hurting nothing."

"If I wanted her I could have had her four hours ago."

It's quiet for a minute. Lorn drinks his beer.

"You know, you've got to let go a little. I don't know what the deal is with you. I've been throwing women at you for six months now. I thought you'd be coming back home free at last. Free to do whatever the hell you want to do. What? You don't like to fuck anymore? Something like that?"

"Maybe that's it Lorn, maybe I don't want to just fuck anymore. I spent the last eleven years married to a woman that I had to beg to have sex with. So I laid pipe to every woman in the office under fifty and all my friends' old ladies. And I found out all my friends had been laying pipe to my old lady and it was a plumber's nightmare. I'm tired of it. I don't want nothing to do with it anymore."

"That's why you and your wife split up? I didn't know; you never said nothing."

"Hell, it was a lot of stuff, from the beginning there was stuff. I didn't want to move to the damn city. She knew I'd hate it, but she was convincing. She'd do this leaning thing, you know, where she'd wrap her arm around my waist and tuck herself up under my wing and smile with those eyes. I swear to you, at first, I'd get hard just looking at her eyes." I could vaguely see Lorn nodding his head.

"She did have nice eyes," he says.

It bothers me, him saying that. I shake it off and say, "It was the leaning thing that really did it. She always got her way. It was pea gravel instead of granite for the driveway. Poplars instead of maples. Teak floors with oriental rugs, not the comfortable wall-to-wall carpet I wanted. The Regal when I would have killed for a Renegade. And worst of all, that damn Cocker Spaniel. Shoot—he would've been lunch for a real dog." I stop, out of breath, and Lorn is laughing and patting me on the back. Then it gets quiet again and I say, "How's your marriage going, Lorn?"

"Shit, Jim, it's different for me and Trina. We got kids, you know?" I don't say anything.

Halfway back to the trailer, Lorn says, "I'll take Deborah home now."

"Yeah, that'll be good."

"You sure, man? You ain't got to even think about it. Just close your eyes and go for it," he teases.

I kick dirt up toward him with my two hundred and twenty dollar boots. "Another time, man."

After they leave, I pull my boots off and start wiping them down with the dish towel. I drink a beer, turn the lights out, and lie on the short, hard bed in the trailer to sleep. As soon as I'm relaxed, I see her, with the stereo cable stretched around her waist and her wet, berry smile. But it stirs me now; it's sexual now. And in the corner of my eye, even in the dark, I see that damn light from the potter's clay lamp. I stand and turn on my light and search for the latest copy of *Life*. I find it under the newspaper on the three by four dining table. I lie back on the hard bed and study the cover. On the bottom right corner it says in small print, "Florida Panther."

The next day, Steve stops by while I'm working on the house. I hired contractors to do most of the work, eighty percent at least. Their job done, the rest, little stuff, is up to me. I'm putting up the railings on the wraparound porch. It's lunch time and it's hot. Steve's wife, Karen, gets out of the truck with him, and she looks instantly out of place. She's one of these tiny women, barely five feet tall and she dresses like the women that work in the bank. She's holding on to Steve's arm and trying not to mess up her shoes as she steps up and over the big mounds of dirt in my yard. I turn back to my work, smiling, thankful that I'm no longer married, and hear her grumbling to Steve as they pick their way over to the house.

"Hey, Steve. Karen. What you know good?"

Steve is a big guy. He's got these huge shoulders and chest, real big bones, and a beer belly that makes him wear his jeans with the waist riding a foot below his belly button.

"Karen has been bugging the hell out of me to bring her over here to see the house. I keep telling her it ain't finished yet, but she can't seem to wait," says Steve.

"Well, now, we want to keep our little Karen happy don't we?" I say, smiling at her. Karen, with her paperback romance mentality, smiles back and blushes. God knows, I wouldn't want Steve to have to go home with an unhappy Karen. I lay the hammer down and take off my nail pouch. "It's still pretty rough looking inside, but I guess you can use your imagination." I caution her about the dust and dirt and lead them around in the house; through the great room, the kitchen, the office, up the stairs to the bedrooms. Actually, it'll be one bedroom and two rooms of, as of yet, undecided nature. She runs her hands over the flat stones of the fireplace, marvels at the high ceilings and the massive size of the exposed beams, taps her feet daintily on the clay tiles of the kitchen floor, and seems all in all pleased with what she's seen.

"Well now, Jim," says Karen. "This really is quite a house."

"Yeah," says Steve. "Now all you need is a lady to share it with. Some lady is going to get real lucky."

Karen looks at Steve, her narrow lips twisting to the side, "This isn't for any lady. This is for Jim. He might not want to share it." Then Karen turns to me looking pleased with herself for being so understanding.

But Steve says, "Yeah, well, looks like it could be a real lonely place, after a while I mean."

Karen laughs, sounds like a child, and says, "Jim? Lonely? I'm sorry, just can't picture it. You think it's true, Jim? Think you'll get lonely here?" She has this flirty look in her eyes.

I cross my arms and lean back on the door facing, "Why would I get lonely, Karen, when your husband's always over here?"

After dark, I shower at the trailer, eat a bologna sandwich, and stand outside drinking a beer. It isn't as dark tonight, but still the moon is small and at the mercy of a few scattered clouds. There's a good breeze now and the corn is noisy and I walk back and forth trying to decide whether or not I want to cross the field. I turn and study my new house to see how it looks from a distance. It looks big, sturdy. I know I'm going to go. It's just a matter of convincing my conscience that there's nothing wrong with it. And there isn't. I'm not going to hurt anybody. No one will ever know about it. I walk to the back edge of the cornfield and start counting off the rows.

I find my place outside her window. She's in the beanbag chair again with the headphones on, but she's not drinking. Her head is resting back on the wall behind her. She looks more like she does when she's working in the store—serious and detached. I never stay long when she's like this. It makes me uncomfortable. She takes the red notebook out of the magazine rack, opens it where the pencil is sticking out of the top, and starts writing. I'm thinking I'm too tired for this tonight and only watch for a few more minutes.

Two days later I'm standing in line at the DMV. I have to get a new license. The Virginia State Troopers don't smile on a Virginia resident holding a Pennsylvania driver's license. This scrawny man behind the counter that reminds me of Gilligan in a blue suit tells me I have to take the written test and hands me the test paper and a pencil. I sit at the edge of one of the two tables in the small room. The four people that were in line behind me move up and a bell rings as someone comes through the door. I start reading the test questions, answer the first three, then get hung up on the next one about stopping distance at forty miles per hour. I look up, working the math out in my head, and there's Sam, standing in the line, right next to the table. She's looking down at me and whispers, "Hi." I get this feeling like something is sucking the strength right out of me and I know I'm blushing because my face is hot. I give her a nod, and try for a smile, but I'm not real sure it comes out as a smile because my cheeks are tight. Looking back at the test, I try to concentrate. I have to read the next question three times before it registers; it's an easy one and I know the answer right away. Pedestrians always have the right-of-way.

Between questions, I glance up to see where she is in the line. My hands are sweaty and I keep shifting the pencil from one hand to the other so I can wipe them on my jeans. She's second from the counter now and I can't take my eyes off of her. She's wearing her burgundy t-shirt and jeans, the only woman in the place, and I can smell her perfume. My mind starts shooting me the freeze-frames I've been collecting of her in my memory and I break off my stare and look around to see if anyone noticed me gawking at her, for an instant paranoid, like someone will figure me out. I realize how stupid the idea is. If you catch someone staring at a pretty woman, you don't automatically assume they stare through her window at night. I laugh inside and sneak one more glance her way. She's at the counter now waiting for Gilligan to return from the back room. He comes out and our eyes catch uncomfortably. I drop my focus back to the test and answer the next question about blood-alcohol levels.

"I lost my license," Sam says.

I hear the tapping of keys on the computer keyboard and circle the answer to the last three questions. I pretend I'm still working on it and strain my ears to listen.

"Name?"

"Samantha Collins."

"Place of Birth?"

"Coos Bay, Oregon."

"Social security number?"

Now there's no one in line but her and I go stand behind her with my test paper and pencil. She's a little shorter than I am and I get this crazy picture in my head—we're slow dancing. The DMV man tells her to come around the counter to have her picture made. I watch her sit in front of a black screen on a wooden stool. She sits straight, no smile, and the flash lights the corner of the room. There's a poster on the wall that says, "Buckle up. It's the law." The DMV man says, "Have a seat. The picture will take a minute." She walks past me and I catch her eyes. They smile at me and she sits where I was sitting at the table.

I hand the man my test and he checks it at the counter. I'm thinking she must be watching me and I almost turn to see, but the Gilligan man holds my test in front of me and tells me I'll have to try again later; I missed five questions. I flunked. And I know she is listening to everything and I want to walk out of there backwards so I don't have to face her. The DMV man hands me a book to study for the next test. I'm twelve years old again, with pimples. I turn, hear him tell her that her license is ready, and she gets up just as I walk by.

"They're not as easy as they used to be, are they?" she says.

"Guess not," I say. "You ever flunk one?"

"Me? No. But I came close last time. It helps to study the little book there," she says and pats the book I'm holding in my hand.

I nod and she walks to the counter. I want to stay and talk, but I feel too stupid.

Lorn and Steve and I meet at Pair's store for lunch about a week later. The night before was a long one of watching for me. When we walk in Sam is breaking pennies out of their paper wrapper into the cash register drawer. She nods to us and asks if I have tried my luck at DMV again. I shake my head "no," smile, and feel my face getting hot again. We sit around the small, white table in back of the store on wobbly, cane-back chairs and eat beans and franks out of the cans with plastic spoons. She sits on a stool at the front of the store behind the counter and stares out the one square of window in the whole place. It's like we aren't even there, like she can't hear Steve's bad pig jokes, and Lorn's accounts of his most recent fights with Trina. Every now and then she turns and I catch her looking at us. Her eyes are pretty when you get to see them, but when we go to the register to pay her, she looks at our hands and the money, not directly at us.

Lorn and Steve have been on me about asking her out. So I try to strike up a conversation when we go up to pay her. Hard as I try, I can't get more than two words and two smiles out of her.

But when I walk out of the store, Lorn and Steve won't let up.

"You should've asked her out," Lorn says.

"I don't think so. That's too much like work there."

But still, they keep at it and take the keys from the jeep and say I'm not going to get them back until I ask her out. I play along and go back in the store. I walk straight to the drink case, grab a Mountain Dew, and take it to the register to pay for it.

"Thought I'd get one to go," I say and put a dollar fifty down on the counter.

She hands me the change and I can tell she has just washed her hair, I can smell it. I nearly lose it. I take a quick step to the side, half of me ready to leave, but the other foot won't budge. She has turned around and is looking back out the window. I try to see what is holding her attention, but all I can see are some old rusty gas pumps that don't work anymore and weeds growing up around them. But then I see Lorn and Steve staring at me through the door.

"Sam? Is that what they call you? Sam?" I ask.

"Yeah," she says and looks at me dead on; nails me with her eyes and it's me, now, that looks out the window. Still looking out the window, I say, "Sam, would you like to go out to Dockside Restaurant with me and eat tomorrow night?" As soon as the words are out I feel brave again and look back at her. Her eyes are brown with this kind of amber glow around the pupils, like the sun setting on a real hot summer night.

"Well, gee," she says, "who can guess if I'd like it or not. I don't really know you."

I think surely she's teasing me. "That's the point of the date," I say. "So I can get to know you and you can get to know me."

A truck goes by outside the store and I hear the horn blow and see Lorn and Steve wave at it.

"I don't date."

It takes me a minute to feel that one out. She isn't joking.

"Why not?" I ask, and slip four fingers knuckle deep into the pocket of my jeans, just to have something to do with my hand. The drink box condenser kicks in and the motor makes a buzzing racket.

"For ten thousand reasons—far too many to list." She's still staring at me, not the least bit shaken by the conversation.

"Give me one," I say.

She looks away and says, "I don't like people very much." She rubs a streak of dust from between a row of keys on the cash register. "Well, I mean, I like them at first, but then it wears off and I don't like them anymore and then, of course, I'm stuck with an irritation that I could easily have avoided in the first place, right?"

I have to think really hard about that one, too. I'm standing there with my mouth sort of hanging open, and I say, "What kind of damn logic is that?"

She smiles as if she is suddenly proud of herself and says, "Mine."

For the last month now, to make me even crazier, she's been changing things. Now, she makes her bed and she bought new sheets. They don't have flowers or lace trim, but they're green with a soft, swirled design. She still drinks wine every Friday night, but now, she never sings and she doesn't cry when she goes to bed. And now, *now*, she sleeps in the raw. The first time I saw her stripping down, I was embarrassed and could barely look out of the corner of my eye. Now, I'm brave. I watch every move she makes and wish she'd make more. She'll sit on the bed some nights and put lotion from a pink bottle on her legs and it's like she knows how damn sexy she is and I think she likes being sexy. Sometimes I'll watch her for an hour or more after she's gone to sleep, hoping that sheet will move, hoping she'll kick it or roll out of it. Something. But it always stays right up under that chin.

Other changes too. She writes in that red notebook more often now. I've got my plan together for that, and there's not much time. The corn is getting dry, and I know it won't be long before the Allens will be out here running the combine through it. Then what? I don't freaking know, but I do know one thing—the whole thing is sex now, from the time I start counting off the rows. Through the whole night, even through the next day, whenever I think about her now, it's sex. God knows I don't want to see the corn go.

Today I'm going to find out what's in that red notebook. I dust off my boots and drive to Pair's store. The air is starting to take on the cool touch of fall. It feels good. Another week and I'll be in my house. The Allens say in another week they're going to take down the corn.

I walk in the store and get a Mountain Dew. When I pay for it, Sam says, "Long time no see." She's wearing this slippery looking lip gloss and I like the way it sets off her teeth when she smiles.

I say, "Yeah," and force my guilty face to smile.

"Got your license yet?" she asks and her face is warmer and friendlier than I've ever seen it.

"No. Haven't had time," I say and I'm trying to think of something to add, but I'm nervous and I can't quit looking at her mouth so I turn to leave. I take my steps long out the screen door and hear it slap shut behind me. She's at work, so I can carry out my plan. If the door to her house is not locked, it'll be simple. If it is locked, it'll be tougher, but still do-able. I haven't really been working on a plan at all, I guess. Just working on getting my courage up, and maybe on shutting my conscience up.

I park the jeep next to the trailer and take off between the rows of corn. I run all the way to her house, straight up the tilted steps onto the porch, and stand looking at the door. After a deep breath, I turn the old cast iron knob to the right and push. Nothing. I turn it to the left and push and the door squeaks on its hinges.

The house has that old house smell, the kind that just never goes away for long. What I notice most about it though is how simple everything is—almost barren. I step through the kitchen. The refrigerator here looks like it's about thirty years old. She's put a flowered vinyl covering on the front door panel and the rest of it is aqua. There are only five rooms and one tidy little bathroom in the whole house. The dining room is dark from the shade of the oaks. On a painted, wooden table there are houseplants spreading out of clay pots and a slat-back chair sits at one end of it. The two rooms at the front of the house are empty. I step into the bedroom. The bed is made and the light is pouring through the window. I sit easy on the bed, careful not to mess up the covers. The room looks smaller from inside. The bed is hard, like mine in the trailer. The red notebook is in the magazine rack. I stand and smooth the covers on the bed, sit in the beanbag chair, and pick up the notebook.

The cover is worn and the pages sort of separate in their fullness. I open it up to the first page. It's a pencil sketch of a landscape. It's been done with a light touch. There are no sharp outlines, nothing bold; it's all shaded and soft and fuzzy. The next five, six pages are pretty much the same and I realize now, she wasn't writing all along, she's been drawing. I flip through it quicker and stop on a certain page that looks extremely familiar. It's a picture of Lorn, Steve, and me sitting around the table at the store. Lorn and Steve are turned toward each other, but I am leaning on my elbows on the table looking straight out, looking at the artist. "She's drawn this thing from memory," I say. I'm amazed. I turn the page. It's a sketch of me, I assume, walking back through the cornfield, with the moon full over my head. I turn the page. It's me, standing outside the light of her window, the moon over my shoulder, full.

"Son of a bitch," I whisper. "Son of a bitch." I study the face she's drawn on me, looking through her window. I'm thankful it doesn't look like a pervert. The eyes are serious. They look concerned.

I turn the page again. Me. In the trailer. Sitting in the chair by the window, holding a beer, looking at a magazine.

Two days later, the combines wiped out the corn. I'm walking along the edge of the field and I see her standing on the other side. She's got something in each hand. She starts walking across toward me. The sun is setting behind her house and she's beautiful, the way she moves across that scraggy field. I'm scared to death of her, of what she might want, or what she might say. Scared I won't be able to look into those brown eyes of hers. But, still, I walk out toward her. To meet her halfway. The torn remains of the corn are scattered out across the field. The long stalks chomped off by the machine are now just spikes that refuse to lie down. I don't know what to think of her, but then I guess she doesn't know what to think of me either. As we get close, I see what she has in her hands and I smile.

We stop in front of each other, near the middle of the field. She holds out a beer for me and I take it and laugh. Hugging a wine cooler to her chest she looks at the ground and says, "Thought we might drink to the harvest," and then she looks up, simple and sweet.

"Can do. Can do," I say. "Come on up to the house."

Shrine

*T*raffic in a small Mississippi town like this is lazy. There are only six or seven traffic lights along the main strip, but it takes forever to get from one end of town to the other. Everyone's so polite—you go, no, you go, no, after you—let's just stop the whole show and let everyone out of the elementary school, all the school buses, all the nice parents picking up, and make sure you let all the walkers cross, for God's sake wait for that little one there, the little one who must've been waited on all his little life because he sure is taking his time now. Christ, how are you supposed to sell houses in a place like this to a lady with no kids, a lady who looks like she's above all this?

I check my lipstick in the mirror on the back of the visor. We're waiting for the straggler to cross. Three cars in front of us, more than a dozen behind, and look at this kid, taking his time. I want to get out of the car, snatch him across the road, and say look—when people are backed up across town waiting on you, you step-to like you got some sense.

"People round here really look out for one another," I say. "Almost no crime." I've been saying dumb things all day. When you're trying to make a sale, you find yourself saying all kinds of insignificant stuff.

"Well. That's something. I suppose that is something," she says, uneasy like, her eyes following the slow kid. She's fighting the process—not wanting to like the place at all—resistant as a dead bolt. She can't afford the kind of house she wants, but she *can* afford a lot better than I'll ever have. It's like she expects someone to chop fifty thousand off the right place, like she's used to people looking at her and saying, okay, then, whatever. She and the straggler there—one and the same—no question. They both feel entitled, both assume allowances to be made on their behalf.

No more worries with her for today, though—back to the Holiday Inn Express we go. We'll have another round tomorrow. Nine houses today, and nothing. Not even interested in the A-frame with the primo landscaping around the in-ground pool. Best thing I've got to show. I'd die for that house.

"You been down to the coast yet?" I ask, dragging along behind a school bus that's feeding diesel fumes into the car.

"Last night," she says.

"Do the casinos?" I ask, because everyone does the casinos.

"It's not Vegas, is it?" she says, and smiles, shaking her head slowly.

I've been showing real estate for five months now and I can't get used to dealing with these people. What do I know about these people? Who am I fooling thinking I can get on with this bunch? How do I know what they want from a house? Give me welders. I know welders. Give me iron workers. I know iron workers. I could find the perfect house for an iron worker. I'll take a construction worker any day of the week. These others—I got no use for them.

About six blocks from the hotel, I pull into the Wal-Mart parking lot. "Not in a hurry are you?" I ask.

"Well—"

"Just need to get a key made," I say, pulling into a parking spot. "Besides, you can tell a lot about a place from its Wal-Mart."

She unfolds herself from the Civic, giving her slacks a little tug, adjusting her blouse, and I beep it locked with the fob. She sighs.

"Where'd you say you're moving from?" I ask as we start across the parking lot.

"Culpepper. Virginia." She's smoothing back her clipped red-blond-brown hair, a chemical blend. Looks decent actually. Got a kind of stock investor look about her.

"Don't know it—is it near Chesapeake Bay? I used to spend summers with a friend in Chesapeake. Her father managed a string of 7-11's there, lived in a little bitty apartment—snuck out a lot at night. Lots of cute sailors in Chesapeake."

"It's pretty far—"

Something catches my eye and I place my arm across her path and say, "Wait." I study the pavement in front of my feet. "God, look. Look right there. You see that?"

She's straining her head toward a garnet-colored stain I'm rubbing my boot across on the pavement.

"What?" she says, and it's the first time I've seen her look alive. "What is it?"

But we're standing in the passer-by lane and a truck is coming, so we move along. "I wonder if—Christ, that would be awful," I say, and then she follows me to the sidewalk, glancing over her shoulder. Then I'm studying the red columns that support the overhang and stretch all the way to the connecting grocery store. "Those three there," I nod toward the first three columns to the right. "Freshly painted. Can't miss that new red."

"Why? What is it? What happened?" She scans the columns from bottom to top.

I really look at her face then. She's pretty somehow, everything I wish I had been at her age, late twenties, tanned, nice hair, tips and overlay on the nails, slacks and blouse she's worn maybe twice in her whole life.

"It was sad around here couple days ago," I say. "Did you hear about it? The old man here?" I nod at the store.

She shakes her head, impatient like.

"He worked here forever; everybody knew him. He was always around. Talking loud. You could hear him all over the store. No family left, except a granddaughter, I think. One of those happy people, smiling. Never seen anybody so happy to push a bunch of carts into a store. A little, short man. Energetic as hell to be so old. They say he used to be an x-ray technician at the hospital before he retired. Wal-Mart's real keen about hiring senior citizens. I think it's because they know they want to keep their hours down. Social security and all that—don't have to worry about them wanting overtime." I glimpse the lady out of the corner of my eye while I look out across the parking lot and then again at the three freshly painted columns. She isn't caring yet. She looks at her watch.

"Yeah, the old man here. See, this guy pulls into the parking lot," I point to the side entrance of the lot, "and he has a seizure. He's in this big old LTD, has this seizure, clamps his foot down on the gas, and runs right over the old man."

"Oh," she says.

I say, "When I think about somebody getting hit by a car, I always think about them getting thrown through the air, you know? But they say the old man just buckled right under that car. Got all fumbled around underneath. Broke him up bad. Killed instantly."

She works her brows into a bit of a frown, shifts from one foot to the other. She really is spectacularly pretty, eyes about three shades of brown.

"Then the car wiped out three of these big columns here," I say. "Ended up pinning a lady against the last one."

She's staring at the columns again.

"Course, the guy had a seizure, couldn't help it. But I heard they're going to press charges on him. Cops said they had warned him once before not to be driving. You know, you can only have so many seizures before they take your license. What is it, four? five? But then somebody else said his mother told him to go to the store for her and that he had, in fact, argued with her about it—about him going to the store when he wasn't supposed to be driving."

She looks at me for a second, then folds her arms across her waist, hugging her elbows like, and nods a bit, looking at her feet. Not exactly indifferent, but close.

"Yeah, sad," I say and look at my feet, too. "Come on." I lead the way to the entrance. I want her to see it, right here in the vestibule, this red satin cross, about four feet high, and flowers, all sitting beside this little card table covered with a white linen cloth and on this table there's a huge, white candle burning beside a picture of the old man and he's wearing his Wal-Mart vest, and his name is enameled on the frame. I didn't know his name until I saw it there: Emmett Krill.

Right here between the mechanical eighteen wheeler ride for kids and the bubble gum machines and the pin-ball machine, this table covered in white with his picture on it, the candle, too, and the big red cross beside it on the floor, and all the flowers. And in front of his picture on the table is this white, leather-bound remembrance book and you sign your name there—to pay your last respects. The signatures in that book—about fifty pages full already—the thing sort of blows you back, the set up here, you're just not expecting it, you know, this shrine to Emmett, right here in the vestibule. But it's a good thing, I mean, because something that horrible should leave a mark on the world for a few days at least.

We stand in front of that table, looking at his photograph for a minute, and I'm trying to decide: sign, don't sign. Because who am I? And who was I to him? I figure he was something to me, you know, must have been because I feel so bad that he's gone and all. So I sign it, lean way over to sign because it's a real low table, like a kid's table, and it isn't very sturdy, and my heart jumps when I think the frame is going to topple, but I catch it, steady it. Without looking, I hand the pen over to her and when she doesn't take it right away, I look up and she's got her hand up to her mouth, biting her thumb nail sort of, and it takes me a couple seconds to realize that what she's doing is trying to hold back a laugh, her face all flushed. And I must've looked miffed as hell because she reaches out with the hand she had just had to her mouth and touches my arm and says, half laughing like, "I'm sorry, but it's just a bit much, just all this, all this right here, *in* here," and she motions with her hands toward the kiddie ride and the gumball machines and the pinball machine, a regular Vanna White, and out it comes, her pent-up laugh.

I put the pen down and there's somebody inside the store watching through the glass. It's a solid stare. It's the old woman who works as the greeter, the lady who always smiles and says, "Hi, welcome to Wal-Mart" and offers you a cart, gives the little ones round smiley face stickers. She's staring at me, with only the glass between us, so close I can see the pink of her scalp showing through her white hair, the softest looking white hair. And her eyes, they're blue, but the blue is so pale you can barely see it. She's got one of those faces with a hundred wrinkles, but like her hair — real soft looking — not dried out and haggard. I look at her name tag for the first time. Belle.

Emmett and Belle. Both of them had outlived their spouses. Belle's husband died almost twenty years ago, they say. Emmett's wife died of cancer five years back. They were a twosome, Emmett and Belle, at least at work. He brought the carts in, she offered them out. They were always smiling at each other, sometimes from across the store. You would see Emmett staring at something, grinning, hands behind his back, and you could follow his stare every time to Belle.

They say she saw the whole thing, the accident, Emmett fumbled about under that old LTD. She was always watching out the window, watching him gather the carts in the parking lot.

She's staring now, at us, and then she looks down at the red cross, looks at the picture that, surely, from that angle, she can't see, and then she just sort of nods and turns away, her hands clutched behind her back, just the way he used to stand, and her fingertips are almost blue she's squeezing them so hard.

This woman comes in with her little boy and he's whining to ride the mechanical frog, but when they step into the vestibule, she freezes and the kid gets quiet. He's still. He looks from the cross, to Emmett, to his mother, to me, then back to Emmett. I can't go in the store—the lady had laughed and Belle had seen. I back out of the way, out the door of the vestibule.

"Where you going?" she says.

"Come on," I say, heading for the car.

"But I thought you needed to get a key—"

"No key," I shout back at her, because one, she's lagging behind, and two, because I'm pissed. I slam the car door after I get in and rest my head back on the headrest. The car smells like her, like whatever perfume it is she's wearing. She gets in and closes her door.

"Look, I'm sorry. I shouldn't have laughed."

"I really don't want to hear your voice," I say, and reach over her knees to dig through the glove compartment. "You really have an annoying fucking voice. Anybody ever tell you that?" I find my copper cigarette case, flip it open, and pick out one of the three tightly rolled joints. I toss the case back into the glove compartment and slam it shut. I dig through the console for a lighter. I rest my head back again, light the joint, and close my eyes for a second.

"Look, this isn't working," she says, her voice carrying a kind of ruffled-feathers edge. "I don't know what you're trying to prove, but it isn't working. You don't sit in the parking lot in broad daylight and smoke a joint. And you can't shock me. Honestly, nothing you could do would shock me." Her face really does get all red and flushed when she's bothered. Like a bad sunburn.

"Fuck you," I say, smiling, and hold the joint out to her. "Toke."

"What the hell is wrong with you?" She crosses her arms tight and stares out the passenger window.

"Take a hit," I say, holding the joint toward her. I reach across with my other hand and find a country channel on the radio.

"I don't want a hit. Put the thing out the window."

"Take a hit or fucking walk back to your hotel."

She snaps her head around toward me. "This gets you fired, you know," she says and her lips are quivering. "You are in the process of losing your job. I just want you to realize that tomorrow at this very hour you will not have a job."

I toke again, close my eyes for a second, and then hand the joint to her. "One little hit for the sake of unemployment."

She ignores the joint and takes a deep breath. "I'll stand outside until you're done making an ass of yourself." She opens the door.

"Then how about going up there to the drink machine and get us a couple drinks."

She rolls her eyes and she's gritting her teeth, the little muscle flexing in her jaw. I watch her walk and then look out across the parking lot in front of me. Carts are scattered everywhere. No one dares to collect them, to take them in to Belle. Of course, it's just a matter of time. They'll have to blow out the candle, close the book, take down his shrine. A new man will eventually gather the carts. And we'll stare at him and watch her stare at him, and, ultimately, we will forgive him for replacing Emmett.

I roll the window down and toss the remains of the joint. The lady opens the passenger door and hands me a generic drink. She lowers her head in, "Are you done?"

"Perfectly," I say.

She climbs into the Civic and slams the door. I sip on the drink and lean over the console toward her.

"What?" she says.

"I am so fucking high, and then there's you. You. Well, you smell like gardenias or something, and your lips are like fucking slippery looking and I swear to you, right now, I would love to kiss you."

She plants her back firmly against the seat, puts a hand between herself and me, and says, "Look, I have to make a life with these people in this town and I sure don't want to start out by everybody seeing me in this dinky car, in a Wal-Mart parking lot, smoking a joint, kissing another woman. I don't smoke pot and I don't kiss women. And I want you to take me back to the hotel now—can you do that?"

I rest my forehead against the steering wheel and start the car. "You'll never have a *life* with these people. You might move here. You might get a couple of them to kiss your ass from time to time, but I *guarantee* you will never have a life with them."

"Whatever." She's hooking her seat belt. We've ridden all over the country today, and now she wants to hook her seat belt.

"Want to drive?" I ask.

She stares hard at me. "No."

I look at my watch. Five till five. "Late," I say, "late. I'm always fucking late for every fucking thing."

"Why?" she asks, and when I don't answer she says, "Just take me to my room first. Take me back to my room."

I zip through town, taking short cuts, impatient with all the polite folks on the main strip. I'm heading in the opposite direction of the Holiday Express, but she doesn't seem to notice.

Three miles outside of town is a paper mill where I used to work re-fabbing boilers. When I pull into the parking lot, she's totally confused. I tear across the gravel lot and spot my guys standing just outside of the security shack. I slow for trucks backing out and pulling off. I sound the horn and pull up in front of my three riders.

"Open your door," I say to her.

"Hey, babes," I holler as they walk toward the car. T. J. smiles, but the others just stare like it's been a hard one.

"Look," says my ruffled passenger, "we really need to get going."

"Get out." I think I'm being damned pleasant about the whole thing. She's sitting there with the door open, staring at me. "I promised them a ride home. Get out." I'm keeping my voice level low; I think I'm maintaining. I pop the hatch for the guys to stow their lunch coolers and hard hats and welding shields.

She steps out of the Civic and I pat the seat for T.J. to sit up front with me. The other two squeeze into the back. The car is leaning toward the passenger side. The smell of gardenias is suddenly replaced with iron dust and sweat.

T. J. says, "You're high, huh, middle of the damn day—what am I going to do with you?"

I look at my dethroned passenger. "Get in."

"Where?" she says.

I look at T. J. and he slides his feet as far as he can toward the front of the car and pats his leg, "Here you go."

She hesitates.

I nod toward T.J. "My brother," I say, introducing him to her. "You staying or going?" I ask and put the car in drive. Now it's very important to me that she climbs into the car, but she just stands there—as if something will change.

T.J. closes his eyes briefly, drums his thighs with his hands, then smiles, saying, "Look, maybe—"

"No, I've got it. Really," she says, her eyebrows compensating as she stoops to squeeze onto T.J.'s lap. Lean as she is, it's still not an easy fit. Her hand clutches the dashboard and her head presses at an angle against the roof of the car.

"If you lean back, you'll have more room," says T.J., and when she doesn't budge, doesn't respond, he says, "Course, we could switch places if you like."

This gets chuckles from the back seat, but when I glance over, the lady's eyes are pooling tears and she's trying hard not to spill them.

"C'mon," I say and lean in against my door. The guys don't get it, don't notice; but she does. Our eyes meet briefly and hers spill and I remember the day I accidentally slammed the kitten in the car door. I pull a Dairy Queen napkin out of the door pocket, hand it to her, and say, "There's a great steakhouse in town. Best ribeye you'll ever get. If we go now we can beat the dinner crowd. Yeah? What do you think?"

She blows her nose into the napkin, nodding, her head still bent at an awkward angle. "Sure. Sounds nice."

The guys send up a unified "yes," but I know—looking at her again, I know—that kitten is dead.

Doubt

*T*his thing happened. No. Many things; in a clump. There's a connection in all of it, must be. But this thing, the thing with the bird, an eagle, golden, which my husband Graham swears is a hawk, but which I have looked at through the binoculars and can verify that it is indeed a golden eagle because it has the feathers down the legs, spiking toward the talons and because when the sky is clear and the bird is gliding loops a half mile above, it catches the sun and is clearly golden brown, and this thing with this bird is the central point in that clump of things which seem connected. It doesn't belong here and I think it is possibly on the endangered list and why it should nest in a half-dead, though tall hickory tree across the road from my house in the middle of Dender, Mississippi when it belongs up high in the Rockies or wherever it is that it belongs—some place high, that seems only right, and with a cooler climate, more isolation—why this is, that it is here instead of where it belongs — is beyond me and it occurs to me now even stranger than it did when I first noticed the bird and wanted to call the authorities because a man was clearing some land across the road, working very close to the tall tree and if this bird is endangered I supposed someone should stop the man. But Graham had insisted I was about to make a fool of myself because it was nothing more than a common hawk. I'd told Graham: that wing span? at that height? way too glorious for a hawk. That was before I'd found the binoculars in the attic and cleaned them up to get a closer look at that great bird. But you see, the fact that even after I handed the binoculars to him and told him to check for himself, the fact that he did look and handed the binoculars back to me shaking his head with "No, uh-uh, not an eagle," the fact that he couldn't even believe it was an eagle after he'd seen the feathers down the legs — for that's the proof fair and square — make me sure of one thing now — that I can never tell him what the eagle did that night.

To be fair to Graham, he's open minded and free thinking about most things, but he could not muster enough imagination in this case to believe that this great bird is a displaced eagle, or, closer to my own opinion, that this eagle, seemingly, had opted for flat land and heat over cool mountain splendor, and when the second eagle came along, a mate to the first, it simply bolstered his objection and he said, "See there? One eagle—maybe. Two—uh-uh."

Normally, I wouldn't wish to insist my opinion on Graham, but you see, this thing the eagle did—it is big—it is big to bursting in me—and if Graham doesn't buy that the bird is an eagle, he'll certainly never believe this. And if there was one person in the world that I thought I could share this with—expecting that to some degree I would be believed—it would be Graham. But now, no.

Truth is, had I not been there, had someone told me something like it, I would think to myself: that's bogus. I would think it was bogus because I've seen movies where things like that happen. I would no more believe it than I can manage to believe that dead Michael Landon is speaking to his family from the grave as was declared on television just the other day. I tend to think about claims like that: that's wishful thinking. And that's how Graham would read this thing with the eagle—he'd claim it was kin to wishful thinking. Yet it was unaccountably real for me, so real I couldn't take a breath for fear of missing some tiny part of it, so real I started to tremble and couldn't even hold the cigarette between my fingers, so vivid even now that I can close my eyes and replay it over and over, the way that bird soared across the sky, the dark profile of it in a sky lit only by streetlights—which is just too much—and right at midnight—which is way over the edge—the scream of that profiled creature ripping the night sky from left horizon to right—and me, in a transfixed state, sitting on the front steps fully conscious that it was all too weird, too familiar, trembling, the cigarette burning on the walkway in front of the steps because I couldn't hold it between my fingers and me whispering, "oh dear God" and had I believed in such it would have been a truly spiritual awakening. Or maybe had I believed in such, God and such, it wouldn't have been so shattering, for I suppose if I believed, it would have seemed like a gift from Him or a soul's progression to Him. Or something. But I didn't believe in such and that—*that*—is why I dropped the cigarette, trembling, not breathing, nor blinking, my spine straight as a steel rod—transfixed—because *that bird at that moment was such.*

Of course, you'd have to know about the phone call before you could really appreciate the thing, but even then it's like a snippet of TV drama. If only Graham would reconsider—say the birds are eagles. If only he could see them again through the binoculars—if he'd just looked closely—and now, it's most likely too late—haven't seen them, that's right, since that night. You see, he'll never believe me. He'll just say that I was in such a high state of anxiety over my mother's condition that anything would have given me the same sense of impending doom—a late night taxi on the street, a cat stalking across the yard, a falling star. And maybe he'd be right.

But, no. The bird, see, it never flew at night—never. I spent many a night on those front steps, smoking, reading, thinking, and that bird did not fly at night—only during the day. And you'd hear the great bird scream in the day, no earlier than ten every morning, leaving the tall tree, the wings spread full, his movement sober, unhurried, looping long, looping higher, until the small birds couldn't reach him. When you start to add it up—that the bird was an eagle with the leg feathers to prove it, that this was a bird that did not belong here, that belonged maybe a thousand miles away from here, that this eagle normally didn't act that way, and that we've not seen the bird or his mate since—all that added up gives some weight to my story. But Graham will smother the facts—he'll say: First, it's an ordinary old hawk. Second, many a bird has taken flight at night. Third, the bird probably has a winter home somewhere else—birds do that, he'd say.

Proof would be if he could have felt it—that tingling, fixed feeling—utterly caught up in that bird's screams, focused on his profile parallel to the horizon, a slow, purposeful pass from my left peripheral vision to my right. But, no, not even that would have been enough to convince—the ironclad proof would have been the knowing that came with that transfixed feeling, the way the eagle became not just a great bird, but a living message, and the way I whispered to it, intuitively, without pause, with a message back as it carried itself out of distance.

It had come screaming into my night, against a sky lit only by streetlights, off to my left as I sat on the front steps, smoking my last cigarette of the day, and with no hesitation, with only a slight turn of my head, I focused on that incredible sight, the cigarette falling as the bird moved straight, not looping, as if in slow motion, its scream straightening my spine, seeming furious in its purpose. And just that quick, out it came: *Mamma, no, not yet—hold on. I'm not ready for this yet*. And these are the things I thought the next second: I haven't bought Graham's suit for the funeral yet, or his shirt, or tie, or shoes; who will fill in for me at work; if it happens now, I'll have to stay up all night getting everything ready—it's such a long drive—I don't want to hold up the funeral; cancer doesn't kill this quick—I must be losing it; the car needs to be washed and vacuumed, the windows—how much does it cost to detail a car?

Then the eagle screamed as it reached the midpoint of my horizon, directly in front of me, across the way, but too close. And again, I whispered, *I'm not ready for this. I'm really not ready, please, please, not yet*, but I wasn't thinking about suits, or the distance to home, or cleaning the car. Then the eagle gave a generous flap of its wings, and I felt it—felt the warmth rush past my face and I gripped my hands together in one great fist, sitting steel rod straight, remembering the heat of Mamma's forehead against my lips, and then the way I'd had to scrape off a coating on the top of her tongue, a tongue like cardboard, a tongue that hadn't met with a drop of fluid in two weeks. Why hadn't the nurses told anyone that it could happen? That the tongue could solidify in its dryness? And the waiting—all day waiting for one moment of recognition—one moment out of the morphine—waiting for the eyes to open and recognize before I traveled the thousand miles back, *Mamma, it's me* at every slight movement, and then, finally, a twitch of the lashes, a shift of the hands across the sheets, across the swollen tummy, and a pitifully polite, "I don't feel very good."

What does one do? What does one say? *I know, Mamma. I know you don't feel good. Rest. Just rest. I'll be right here.* Not *sleep Mamma*, but just *rest*. Only the rest wouldn't come and there was nothing in her but moans, and tears at the corners of her closed eyes, and stiffening and shifting until I'd reached over to push the white button, the boost of morphine, pressing my lips to her hot forehead. And the sweet, the absolutely gorgeous silence, as her body relaxed and the forehead smoothed under my lips.

And remembering this, the feel of her forehead as it smoothed under my lips, and seeing, hearing the eagle scream across the horizon on my right by then, my spine gave into a slump, the fist of my hands relaxed on my lap. *Never mind, go. Go, it's all right.* And the eagle's wings beat steadily and yet the air was still. Silent. I sat staring after it, waiting for the phone to ring. And (maybe I saw this or maybe my head was zonked at the time) I heard a rustle beside the steps where the mums were beginning to bud out for the fall. There, working under the mums, under the leafy mulch, was a snake—a maize color, a color snake I've never seen, the color of a rarely used crayon—and I leaned to see the head, it being no more than a foot and a half long, because I thought it could be, most probably was, a lizard, and so I watched how it moved and saw the head and, no—it was a snake. I moved my feet further away from the edge of the step and the phone rang inside, making the house sound hollow. I took a deep breath and stood to go in, one eye on the snake as its tail disappeared under the mums, and looked at my watch—five minutes after midnight.

"She's gone," my sister said. "Barry just called from the hospital." And I almost said: *I know*.

It was a clump of things, though. Not just the eagle, but the eagle does seem central. And what sticks out in my mind is the three of us, my sister, my brother, and I, sitting in the hospital room on my last visit only a couple of weeks before, discussing the funeral arrangements, mostly debating open or closed casket, whispering because we weren't sure how much Mamma could hear. My brother had called me when she first started being *not aware*, said, "I came and sat with her pretty much all day, and she didn't wake up the whole time. I just sat and held her hand and read the paper." And I had thought how the hell could he sit with her, knowing she's dying, and read the paper? And yet all day on this last day of my last visit with her, and I knew it would be my last visit because she was dying fast and because of the thousand miles I would soon put between us, and still all day my brother, my sister, and I had entertained her guests in her hospital room, welcoming them, carrying on conversations that had little or nothing to do with her, each of us slipping a glance her way from time to time. And then, there we were, whispering about funeral arrangements.

Again my brother surprised me, "It won't be so hard, I don't think, when we see her in the casket. We'll know she's not there, that she's in heaven, that that's only her body and that she doesn't hurt anymore. "And I'd sat there, nodding my head along with my sister, all the while thinking *jeez'um, he really believes this* and I looked at my sister and I could see that she believed it, too, and so I'd sat nodding, trying to make myself look as if I did, but I knew that I'd have to cope with this dying in some different way.

It had reminded me of the time, a mere month before, on a visit I made while Mamma was still at home, but right after she found out about the cancer. She'd said while propped up in her bed in the spare room, "Pray for me. But not that I live." She had not the least bit of fear of dying. But she was petrified of the pain she'd have to endure before she got there. And me, saying, "I'll pray. That God will be merciful and tender with you." And we'd held each other, me wanting with all my being for there to be this heaven for her, some blissful reward for her, seeing as how she'd spent her whole life sacrificing for one, was counting on it now as surely as day brings light and night the moon.

As soon as the call came from my sister, I hung up and called Graham. His job had taken him out of state and he had to make a five hour drive home. I supposed there was part of him that couldn't help thinking: thank God it's over. And Graham believed in God and such and it occurred to me then how odd it was that we'd never discussed it.

Later, while repacking Graham's suitcase, I found a thick letter, folded in half, five pages long.

"What's this?" I asked and he took it from me and opened it, reading, flipping a few pages, as if he needed to refresh his memory.

"Just a letter from this woman I met in the laundromat there. We talked about things."

"In the laundromat?" I said, because Graham doesn't know laundry, laundromats, detergent, washing, folding, bleaching, sorting—these are things that Graham doesn't do.

"Yeah. We talked. She's a nice lady. We talked about you, how hard it was for you right now—your mother, the cancer, all that."

I nodded and flipped through the five pages of letter—*I'll pray that God will fill your heart the way he's filled mine. That he'll do for you what he's done for me. Before God, I was a lonely, empty soul . . . .*

I put the letter on the dresser and busied myself packing, looking up at Graham's reflection in the bathroom mirror as he shaved. An attractive man, a steady man. I thought: *if God's done so much for that woman's loneliness, how much more could Graham do.* There's always been a definite connection in my mind between religion and sex. It's all about filling needs, making deep, emotional connections. I had to wonder what made her write that. To Graham. Had he claimed loneliness, an empty soul? And I went from reading that letter to visualizing Graham with some passionately needy woman, replenished, naked under hotel sheets, an FM channel casting softly from the television.

Then I remembered the eagle, and took a quick breath, ready to tell him, "Graham—" but he wouldn't believe me. He'd smother the facts. Hadn't even been able to admit that it was an eagle. Tiredly, I wandered outside and sat on the steps. The missing of her was deep and absolute, more profound than I could have comprehended.

I felt like I was on the wrong side of a shoreline. There was a gulf of difference between me and them, all of them—Graham and his letter writing witness, my brother, my sister, my newly deceased mother, all fixed solid on some opposite shore, a shore they made look right—me shaky on this other, the brick and mortar of the steps seemingly foreign, the mere illusion of solidity—and just when I think I will splinter into a zillion insignificant pieces, my incredulous eagle soars across the horizon, like a pull on a zipper, and me its only witness.

Seventh Day

The sixth night, ungodly stiff, jeez your back, the mattress hard as a church pew, the young ones stabbing your kidneys, your breasts, with elbows and heels, or breathing all over your face and if there's one thing you can't tolerate, the thing heading the list, Sayward Tyne's great list of things not to be tolerated, it is that: the hot breath of a sleeper competing with yours, never mind that it's coming from your own wee one. There's a draft that's got your nose all runny now and the cover's bunched about the two children, clenched under arms and legs curled about in it, blankets worn thin years ago, and now the ear's starting to ache. Ear's aching, nose running, cold, stiff, the pain in the back, a permanent sort, nothing to feel good about—not here, not now— 'cept maybe that they're too young to know what's going on and they like new places and they ate thrice today and they're sleeping warm.

You've fucking done it to yourself again, Sayward, the fucking princess of fucking up. But no, he needed it, the son of a bitch, needed a good jolt this time. I'll not be married to the man, him knocking me about, fucking strangling me this time, and it was the red marks there about my neck that earned me the week in the safe house. You should have seen old Sayward, running her fingers rough along those marks all night that night, making sure they didn't go away, 'cause they were too good to be true is all. Marks are hard to come by—he's usually careful about leaving any marks. That's why he likes to hit the back of your head and yank you about by the hair. I'd rather he broke the nose, really, 'cause then you can wear it up front, point to it, say see what the son of a bitch did to me. But it's hard to explain a fucking lump on the head, no broken skin, no bleeding, no broken bones, no visible bruises. Actually, she could hold her own with Nathan most times, and he only cut loose on her when she got up in his face and accused him of fucking about, or bitched at him 'bout his drinking. And truth be told, I'd done my share of shoving and slapping. Busted his lip good one night. But he had it coming this time. There was a definite lack of balance, now, with him winning every time and fucking around, you know he's been fucking around, and staying out till dawn some nights and not wanting to touch you, and by god there aren't a handful of men that he works with that wouldn't give a week's salary to be touching old Sayward. They've said as much and he's heard them when she used to work a man's job, a real job, side by side with them. But that was before the accident.

Well, you can't have it, can't let yourself be a fucking coward, gotta stand apart there and say well fuck you and your house and your fucking temper and your drinking and your fucking whore whoever she is and you'll not have the pleasure of touching me again. He can just go jack himself in a corner. Cause you're not nothing, you know, Sayward, you're still fine. I've kept myself fit, I have, running after these kids here. And the accident hadn't slowed her down too much, even though there were limitations. Good to go—could go a round with any man, I could. But Nathan's an ox, got the brain of an ox, too, but got the heart big as one most times and that's what you're missing, Nathan's big arms wrapping you up while you sleep, laying here, cold and stiff, in a house that don't belong to you nor to anyone you know even.

Safe house, my ass, the car parked out front, all he's got to do is ride by and see it. Not a soul here to keep him from busting through that door, knocking the life out you, and hauling off the kids. A cop that drives by with his spotlight facing the house twice a night. I know because I can't sleep nights. No curtains on the window here by the bed—there's your draft—and I keep looking at those black sheets of glass thinking maybe a face will pop up. How safe is that? Could shoot a person sleeping right here in this bed through that window. What's to stop you? A chain link fence out back that any little thief could hurdle?

The first night here, there'd been a light flashing about in the yard inside that chain link fence and when she knelt beside the window, squinting into the darkness, she saw it was a man prowling about with a flashlight. Your heart takes a hit of adrenalin when you see the likes of that, and Sayward freaked and screamed into the den of the house and the two black girls that were co-occupants of the house snuffed out a joint they'd been sharing, saying what you talking 'bout girl? Each grabbed one of my elbows and pulled me down to the floor—what you see Sayward? And the one said to the other, Nicole, go look out back? Nicole stared wide—suck what? And the bossy one rolled her eyes—nigga, please, get your fucking claws off me. I go.

Course it was only a policeman walking the premises with a flashlight, checking the windows 'cause there was a new girl in the house. Sayward, the new girl. The two black girls started pumping perfume in the air and when they opened the door and let the officer in, I told him—you scared the shit out of me 'cause my old man said if I took the kids and left he'd kill me and I knew you were him, or one of his friends.

You should have seen the look on the black girls' faces—your old man got a contract out on you? The lady brought you here didn't say nothing 'bout no contract on you. Well, that's it—I ain't staying in no house with nobody that's got no contract on 'em. You tried to explain to them, not a contract really, he only said it was so. But the bossy one was pulling a pair of jeans over her fat hips in a flurry of movements, saying Your husband a white man? White men say they gone kill you, I don't fuck around with 'em. Black men say it all day long—in one ear and out the other—abut a white man—ever heard of a serial killer that was a black man?—no, white mens be serious talking about fucking you up. Then, let's go, says the bossy one to the other who was dressed already. They headed out the front door, big purses flopping against their hips and I'd stood in the door and watched them walk down the sidewalk to the street, mumbling to themselves. Fuck 'em. I crawled back into the bed with my kids.

You can't sleep after something like that and a window like that right by the bed and all. But it didn't matter anyway, 'cause an hour after they left, the lady in charge of the house was bringing them back. Seems the cops had picked them up and called her to come get them at the station. So the doorbell's ringing an hour later and you get up and look out the front window. There they stand, arms crossed, the bossy one rolling her eyes at me peeping at her through the window. And old Sayward was nervous about opening that door, I can tell you, 'cause the look on the lady's face, she was pissed as two cats with their tails knotted agether. And then she's on you like white on rice—what on earth did you tell these girls?—well I hope you know you have scared them silly—you have truly caused a disruption here. And you want to know what the fuck right this bitch thinks she has to be up in your face, pissing and moaning like that—this is a safe house, ain't it? Aren't they in danger, too? Or no? They just hanging out here, is that what you trying to tell me? You should oughta be bitching at them, lady, they're the ones broke the house code—leaving without permission—leaving at night. You should have told me, she goes, you should have told me of the death threats. It does make a difference, you see. Tomorrow, you'll need to see if you can move your car into the back yard. I don't know if it'll fit through the gate back there, but it's not good for it to be sitting out front.

The two girls sat themselves down on the loveseat in the den. The bossy one grabbed the remote and turned the tv on. Loud. The lady of the house left and I locked the door behind her. I turned, stared. The quiet one flung a finger toward me without taking her eyes off the tv—you stay the fuck on your side of the room—don't want you nowhere near me—I ain't taking no stray bullet aimed at your narrow ass.

Seventh Day | 135

The next morning, there we stood, Sayward and the lady of the house, standing behind the big beige Impala, staring, their hands cupping their elbows, perplexed. The Impala was wedged just inside the gate, the side mirrors the only thing stopping it from going through. It would have been the perfect place for it, the lady said, what with the vines growing all up around the fence that way. We sighed defeat and I re-parked the car in the front where it's been all this time. I'd been told the rules—no contact with anyone for seven days—no phone for seven days—no leaving the house for seven days—no leaving the house after seven days unless you let her know where you're going—no leaving the house at night—no male visitors—no liquor, drugs. There was an attorney affiliated with the house. You were to make arrangements for restraining orders before the seventh day—no need to leave the house—the attorney would come there.

What are your plans—do you have any plans? Now, there's the gist of the fuck-up, I suppose. Not a plan one when I left the day before, only to get away with the kids before he got home. Be packed and ready when I get home, Nathan had said that morning. I don't give a fuck where you go, but you ain't taking them kids. And you ain't staying here. What do you do? You got to one up him. A choice like that—nothing to do. You got to regain an ounce of control over the situation. Course the marks get you into the safe house, and thank christ for them, 'cause there's nowhere else, her parents off somewhere in a Winnebago—no childhood home left—they'd sold it for the Winnebago and given up their roots to go traveling about, playing host and hostess at camping resorts all over the country and into Canada. They wouldn't want to be bothered in their happy retirement by the likes of this. You wouldn't for the world bother them, either. Most of your friends are men you used to work with, men you and Nathan used to work with, and they were sure to take his side and you couldn't just go off living with some man who might take you in, Sayward, not with the kids and all. Course, the lady here says put him out, the courts will give you the house, you've got the kids to raise. But it's his house, you tell her, his grandmother's old place—can't be right to take over his grandmother's old place. And if you did, if by chance you talked yourself into doing something that low, the place is fifteen miles out in the boondocks—how the hell do I get back and forth to work every day with that gas guzzling monster out front and its bald tires—and how do I keep insurance on it— with the kind of job I can get, my back busted and all, not being able to work a man's job anymore— I'd be working minimum wage, you can bet, just enough to pay the child care for watching the kids while I work. Then how am I suppose to pay the electric bill and get food and lady don't talk food stamps to me, don't go there. He'll have to pay child support, the lady interrupts. He'll have to make sure to keep insurance on the kids and you'll most likely get the house and he'll pay you child support. Then you look at her in her maize power suit with her little earrings to match and pumps sure to be leather and you know she hasn't got the foggiest, not the foggiest idea what Sayward is talking about. Lady, she says, we ain't got insurance to begin with. And it's all we can do to pay for what we got right now. We're just scraping along the bottom here. And you think he's supposed to be able to do all he's doing now, plus find himself a place to live? Look, I say to her—and here's Sayward now, making up her mind, knowing damn well what she's going to do when her seven days are up—you lose everything, maybe you end up like me, just scraping by. Maybe you won't wear that nice yellow suit and leather on your feet. Maybe you'll wear tennis shoes and jeans from K-mart and pull your kids out of that private school you probably got them in. Me, lady, us, me and Nathan—that's where we're at right now. Any lower down, any harder than that and we go to stealing what we need. Got me? She didn't get me. Just blagged on—there's government sponsored day care centers based on how much you make—there's government sponsored housing—there's welfare, for christ sake, there's Medicaid. Give me a fucking break. Like any of it's a choice to make. You don't choose that shit, fuck sake. You're shoved into it—it's not a viable option. Leave a home in the country for the projects? Put your kids in free day care? Choices, my ass.

Course, Nathan, he's got the advantage—he knows it. He's got a place, he can make the money. He can provide. Only once in my life could I say that—only once has Sayward felt on top of things—and that's when Nathan taught her to weld. Then we worked the construction hotsheet over as a team. I did the spot welding, he did the pure burn. We worked up high, 'cause the heights didn't bother us, and you're safer there, you know, no one dropping shit on you from above, no one pissing on you. And for eight months, it felt good, going home tired as Nathan, bringing home a paycheck equal to Nathan's, fucking proud I was to hear him say I could keep up with the best of 'em out there, light on her feet walking them beams in the air, ever see anybody walking tip-toe 'cross a beam in Red Wings? he'd ask about and point to her. Never seen nothing like it. And christ, they could fuck those nights, tired as they were, they went at each other, and teased each other up on the beams by day. He'd come up behind her, ten floors up they'd be, press her against a steel column and rub against her till the entire crew on the ground was whistling and hollering up at them. He'd reach around front and squeeze her breasts through her coveralls and she'd reach behind and grab his ass. The supervisor would break up the audience on the ground and shout up to them to save it for when they got home—they weren't getting paid to fuck around on the job. Then at home, the kids in their room asleep, they fucked with the same intensity they'd felt ten floors above the ground, fucked like they had a fucking audience.

But that was forever ago. Before the fall. And now you're fucking stretched on the edge of a super-size cot with the kids, in the barest of houses, a nice house, but nothing homey 'bout it, with one small toy box full of broken toys that the kids are already bored with, a small shelf of books with pages missing and pages scribbled on, and you with insomnia from day one, waiting for the morning, day seven, so you can make your call, tell the man your coming home, but things have got to change. He should be 'bout ready to buckle by now. Six days and nights, no word from you, no word 'bout you or the kids, wondering maybe if he'll ever see you again. He should be past the anger now. Should be into that sort of numb, weepy stage. Should be ready to break. And Sayward, you got to do it, got to break him every now and then, 'cause if you don't, he gets too big, too damn tough-hearted to even touch. Tomorrow night wc'll sleep together again. He'll want me, maybe as much as he used to before the accident.

It's the fucking fall that ruined it all and, sure, you tried to sue the sons-a-bitches, but they blamed the thing on Nathan and then banned husband-wife teams from working together as if the whole thing was the result of a distraction. But really it was my own fault, a slight forgetfulness on my part. Nathan and I were working cross the beams, eighty feet up, cutting across from one to another over a thick plank of plywood. It meant latching on with your safety harness and disconnecting again every time you had to move back across a beam. It was a lot to remember. And Nathan and I shared that plywood. Sometimes he had to move it to cross to a different beam. When I fell, he'd just moved the plywood. I knew it, had seen him do it, but didn't remember till that one foot was out there in the air and then it was too late. I'd disconnected to move across to Nathan and then I was free falling. I was lucky really, could have fallen the whole eighty feet, could have burst open like a tomato on the concrete below, but I landed into an empty scaffold on top of a bucket about twenty feet down and swayed back and forth on there till they lifted me down in a basket using the crane. Then came back surgery—a broken vertebra, but no spinal damage—wiring the pieces of bone back together. Then therapy with the motto "chase the pain, but don't catch it." And pain pills that made me want to sleep all the time. And hired help to watch the little ones while I recuperated. And we ate through the savings then and sold the boat. Three months later, here comes Sayward's medical release—can return to work—light duty. That means tool shed attendant, fire watch maybe, front dispatcher. It meant squat. There isn't a construction site in the world you can work on once you answer that little question on the application that says have you ever received an injury to your back. End of me doing man's work. End of me doing anything that will make a decent living—the classic non-skilled American female fuck-up—dysfunction to follow. Then the law suit fell through after the lawyer had Nathan full of hope for a settlement close to five-hundred thousand. Fuck it. A man spills hot coffee all over himself and gets millions. I spill from eighty feet up and get squat. Story of Sayward's life.

It was also the end of great fucking as far as Nathan was concerned. Not that I couldn't, or that I can't, but Nathan kept running into new limitations and it hindered him. Couldn't do the grind any more, the slow belly grind atop him, just couldn't get her back flexible enough for it, with him reaching and squeezing her small breasts in his hands, pinching her pips till she winced and smiling at her, biting his bottom lip, all tough, giving all to Sayward, sweaty, strong Sayward, the old Sayward, full of sex, bring it on she was, but she couldn't bear it now, not that, nor the way he fucked her with her knees bent and pressed against her breasts, her feet on his chest, holding the drunk bastard steady while he slopped in and out of her, fucking acrobats they were, but fuck, she wasn't Gumby, you know, she couldn't limber up to it is all, christ, what fucking difference it makes, it made, for them though. Ah, but she'd liked it, that wide meaty chest, her wee painted toes pressing into him there, the cool drops of sweat that would fall from his hair to pool on her belly, the feeling of being racked, his weight pinning her tight, the way he'd growl, growl loud like a grizzly when he came, one long fucking growl and christ she loved that moment, Sayward craved that moment and she never ever wanted to share that kind of moment with anyone else but him since him. No, only him, you really, really only want to fuck him, all these years and christ he knows every inch of Sayward, he does, knows how her body works, and you think about him not being happy with you anymore, you know, you think about all these things, but you can't help but think it, the way you have to guzzle him down your throat just to bring him to life now, Sayward rubbing about, long smooth legs, up and down against him, rubbing just so against him, just so he'll feel a nipple stiff or feel Sayward wet, Sayward needy, and for what use christ sake, 'cause she'll have to do it, have to resort to it, the long winded guzzling act, guzzle, fucking guzzle, just to feel him hard, and christ the chore of it, the fucking jaw-ache of it all, but what gets you is that it used to do with just a leg, the smooth fucking leg and shit the times you've come out the bath and had the iron waiting you—no guzzle, no leg, just fucking anticipation. But that was before and what's done is done and I can't change that. What's there to do?

You sit up slowly in the bed, and move to the door. The black girls are giggling from the den and you smell the pot burning. They see me come out and roll their eyes. Look at them looking at me and them all dressed up in tight dresses, the cleavage blooming above the necklines. What time is it, I ask, and the bossy girl says it's about time to go and she and the quiet one slip off the love seat, snub out their joint and head to the door. I look at my watch. Two a.m.. Late start tonight, ladies, I say, and the door shuts behind them. Every night, the same thing. You can't figure the deal with them.

I grab my cigarettes off the counter in the kitchen. About out. Yeah, Sayward, time to go home. You know when you run out of cigarettes, girl, it's time to go home. Five dollars in my pocket. Just enough gas to get there. Maybe you shouldn't call first. Maybe you should just show up. No, Sayward, you gotta call. He's gotta ask you to come back. You can't let on that you're gonna anyway. She goes out the back door, sits on the cool concrete step, a light bulb blazing above her head. She lights her cigarette. It ain't so bad. Maybe it'll be good again. There's a fogginess to the back yard around her, the grass needing to be mowed, a smelly garbage can beside the steps, the lid on the ground beside it. She walks down the steps, picks the lid up from the ground, and places it firmly on the trash can. That's better, now. Nothing worse than old stinky garbage. Another of those things not to tolerate on Sayward's great list. She walks into the yard a ways, the grass wetting her feet, and she balances on one foot trying to pinch up little pieces of grass with her toes. She takes the last puff of the cigarette, watching the smoke as it hits the foggy air. She shivers and turns to go back into the house. There's an explosion, and the feel of a hot nail catching the edge of her upper arm. She'd felt the gown tug across her arm. And the instinct to fall came right along with a sudden loss of balance, the coward's instinct to lay down. To not move. She heard a car start up and then she heard, clearly heard, a man speaking excitedly. And what Sayward heard was either *Got her* or *It's not her* and then the sound of the car shifting gears, first, second, third. Even before she lifted herself from the ground there, she was struggling for recall—Got her or It's not her? Which, dammit, cause it makes a fucking world of difference. And you decide on the last. It's got to be the last.

What a mess, it is, fucking blood running down off the tips of her fingers. Sayward, you've gone and done it this time, but no, it's not so bad, just like a bad cut is all, right across it went, thank god. Just hold the towel there a while; it'll be alright shortly. You change out of your gown, is what you can do now, and you wait. Wait for the crack of dawn and then you call and then you go home. Enough of this place. There's not one bit of hope in this place. Not one bit of hope in anything except going home. He'll be different now. It'll be good now.

At the first light of day, I do it—I call. One ring. That's all it takes for him to answer the phone and he's all baby, what are you doing to me, I've been dying here, fucking going nuts here, I didn't mean it, never meant for you to leave, christ, you know me better, don't you? Baby, shit, you gotta come home, I'm sorry, I'm sorry, I can't make it without seeing my babies, I miss the hell out of my babies, and you, goddamn, what's going on in your mind? There you go, Sayward, getting nuts on me—fuck, baby, I love you. Damn, you know I love you.

And then, it'll be better, baby, yes, and I ain't fucking around, why the hell do you keep thinking I'm fucking around, I don't need nobody else, Sayward, you know that.

When the kids wake up, you tell him, you'll come home. You guess. And that is that, and it was better than I ever thought. Broke him, you did, that attitude of his. The great balancing act's not so wopsided anymore.

Wake the little ones. Dress them. Where's your sock, Boo, I thought I had everything right here? Well, never mind then, never mind. You want to go see Daddy? Yeah! Let's go, c'mon, hustle, hustle, gotta hurry. Wash the faces. Brush the little bits of teeth. And you there, Sayward, you there in the mirror, you still got it, you do, and he'll hold you tonight. And maybe before tonight. Maybe even when you walk in the door.

You pull into the drive and park the car and he swoops up Boo and you carry the toddler and he can't say a word, not one thing, his lips are quivering just so, this big ox of a man with his lips trembling, and you want to kiss him, kiss him for the longest, longest time and at the door, he lets Boo in first and then takes the toddler in and tells Boo to take him in the living room, turn on the TV. And, now Sayward, he turns to you, just he and you on the porch outside the back door, and he reaches with a slow hand behind his back, tugging, and with a steady arm brings it out and to you, his 9mm, right up close to your forehead and with the other hand, he grabs a handful of hair in back of your head. Down, Sayward, fucking down you go, on your knees, you will never do anything like that to me again, you hear, and you're sure the gun is cutting into your forehead, you've never had anything pressed into your head quite that hard before. And for about twenty seconds you think he's absolutely capable of pulling the trigger. Don't fuck up, Sayward, don't do one single thing to fuck-up. But there's nothing else to do—I reach up and with the back of my hand, I press softly on his extended arm, smiling at him, and the gun doesn't press as hard against my forehead. With my other hand I touch the side of his leg feeling his calf muscle tense under his jeans. I reach up to his belt and hook my fingers over it and pull hard to stand back up and he's letting me, got his fingers in my hair, still pulling downward, but he's letting me up and that's all I need. 'Cause you're fucking strong you are, fucking bulletproof, don't mind that the knees are weak as noodles. Up, and wrap the arms around his neck, that thick neck, hot on your lips, the shoulders solid. You will never do that to me again. No, Nathan, never. I would never. And look at him now all broke, all leaning on Sayward, crushing the air out her with his arms.

Gone

The man on the car radio talks about the grey whales off the coast, they're making their pass. I listen to him ramble on—he's aiming for the tourists, I know—how the whales only make two runs by the Oregon coast a year, once between December and January, when they move south, down from the arctic waters off Alaska to the birthing grounds in the warm waters around Baja. Then, sometime around the first of spring, they head back north.

I'm driving dead into the sun, but there's a garbage truck in front of me, so I'm riding in its shade. Been watching this guy hanging onto the back of that truck—a blond guy. What a job—but look at him—moving like he's part of that truck, like he's following the lead of a dance partner. The radio man yabbers on about the whales. The northerly migration is the most exciting, he says, because the mothers are returning with their calves and the pops are proud and aggressive, more likely to pitch and roll. He mentions Yaquina Head. A good viewing area, he says. That's it; I'll ride up there and spend the day. Yaquina Head is only about a two-hour drive. I've lived here all my life and never seen the whales. I'll go to the apartment, change, grab the camera.

I'm losing the shade of the garbage truck—let it get too far ahead—so I press on the gas to catch up. This garbage truck man is maybe twenty-five, tall, slim, but not too. He's wearing this black leather duster that's flapping in the wind and when the truck takes the turns he leans out diagonally, into the curve. His knees bend in with the dips in the road and he pulls himself upright again with a suggestive move of his hips. He's on stage. A regular Elvis. He signals with a black-gloved hand to the driver and the truck slows, edging close to the curb. Swinging out and down, like a hawk diving, he swoops up a bag of garbage, and with no awkward movements, he swings it into the truck.

We get to a four-way stop and the garbage man stares at me, his back pressed against the truck now, one hand holding a metal grip on the side just above his head. He smiles. Beautifully. And look at me. Smiling back, for Christ's sake. As the truck starts through the intersection, the garbage guy cocks his head a bit, and with his free hand, gives a little wave, a mere flick of his wrist. With my eyes fixed on the truck, on this garbage man, I pause briefly at the stop and then continue. There's a horn. Something says hit the brakes. A car to my left jerks to a stop. It was his turn. I shift into reverse, back up just a little, the driver behind blowing the horn, paranoid that he's going to be hit. The car on the left pulls off slowly. I give an apologetic smile and mouth the word "Sorry" as it starts by, but when it's directly in front of me, there's the young driver, looking straight at me, angry, and shooting me the bird with all his might. So now I feel stupid for mouthing "Sorry." I look both ways and continue through the intersection, but the garbage truck is gone.

At the apartment, I turn on the stereo and change into jeans, dig the camera out of the closet and realize the batteries are probably no good. Haven't used it in the last year, or two. Maybe three. No sweat—they got those little cardboard ones at the drugstore. It's next to the gas station and I've got to stop for gas anyway. And the bank. Can't go off without cash. I grab the checkbook, the keys, and smile at the empty apartment as I pull the door closed. I clocked into work this morning, stayed fifteen minutes and clocked back out. Said I was sick—had to go. I couldn't handle it today. It's not like I don't have sick days due me.

After I gas up, I pull up to the drugstore and there's only one parking place left in the front. There's an old white Mustang parked on the left of it, only he's parked right on the line. A blue Toyota is parked on the right and I have to think for a minute—is there enough room? Yeah, sure. I pull the Civic into the tight spot, congratulate myself that I didn't hit anything.

The smell of sausage cooking smacks me when I go in. The cardboard cameras are on a shelf behind the lady at the register. "Going to see the whales?" she asks—guesses really—when I pay. I nod, take my change, and wait for her to put the camera in a bag. She's slow. When I get outside, I see something on my windshield. A parking ticket? I snatch the piece of paper out from under the windshield wiper. "Park a little closer to somebody next time, Asshole!"

I pull into the second bay at the bank's drive through, scribble out a check, and slip it into the money tray. A woman's voice says, "How are you today?" through the three- inch speaker on the column beside the car, but I can't see her because there's a van in the first bay. I say, "Fine," but I know she can't hear me because there's a button next to the speaker labeled Push to Talk. The van pulls away and I look toward the woman in the window of the bank. She's busy with something that I can't see—my money, I hope. She looks out at me, smiles, and dangles something in the window in front of her. "Dog biscuit?" she asks through the speaker. I smile, shake my head "no," and she shoots my money off to me. A man pulls up in the first bay, a miniature collie stepping all over him, excitedly. I try to remember when they stopped giving suckers to kids.

I head out to Highway 101. As usual it's bumper-to-bumper tourists. I merge in behind a tan Saturn with Utah plates. It's a beautiful drive up the coastline with a lot of scenic lookout points. The driver of the Saturn is obviously not used to driving the steep curves and he's overcompensating with his brakes. Two small girls, two little blond ponytails swishing back and forth, sit close on the back seat. There is a loud four-wheel drive truck behind me and when it backs off, I can see two young men, each hanging a bare arm out the side windows, but when it gets close, there's only chrome bumper and huge shocks in my rear view mirror, oversized super-swamper tires in my side mirror. It's getting six miles per gallon, is what I'm thinking. They're towing a forest green dune buggy on a trailer, its whip antenna topped by a bright orange flag. I can see the trailer only when we're taking the sharp turns, the kind that throw you back the way you were coming. The truck hangs close, the driver sure of the road—locals, anxious to get to the dunes.

    I try to concentrate on the Saturn in front of me. The two little girls turn around in the back seat of the car. The sun is dead in my eyes now. Once again, I've left my sunglasses at home. My eyes are squinted into narrow slits and I'm pushing up in the car, trying to get into a position high enough for the sun visor to work for me. I put my hand up, trying to block the glare. They're twins, I can see now. I smile at them and wave my fingers from the steering wheel. They wave back with hands cupped tight, just moving their fingers up and down. I wave again and the girls look at each other, full throttle on the giggles. When they look back, one of them sticks her tongue out at me, which she follows with a smile. I stick my tongue out and smile, too. I make a series of faces at them, all that I can remember from childhood, and then, heck with it, make up some new ones. They're getting really boisterous now, on the verge of getting in trouble, because Mom there just turned around and gave them the evil eye. I don't care if you do get in trouble, I say out loud. I'm not going to stop until you do. I let go of the wheel for a second and make the turned-up pig nose and they go nuts, bouncing up and down on their knees in the back seat. The Mom glances worriedly at the Dad. I grab the camera out of the bag beside me and pretend I'm taking their picture. Of course, I'm just fooling—sun's all wrong—it wouldn't develop. But it sets off the last round that flips Dad's switch. Now, while he's trying to negotiate the curves with one foot on the brake, he turns his head as far as he can towards them, points a finger over the front seat, and the girls turn around, sitting so only their ponytails show. I see the shoulder harnesses of the seat belts being pulled toward them and I know they're fumbling with buckling themselves in, as instructed no doubt.

The truck is not backing off. I tap the brakes a few times. The bumper keeps showing up in my rearview mirror and when I look out the side mirror there's the massive tires. A bowling ball following a grape. There's a Super Sammy's Quick Stop up on the right. I pull in and let him have it—the whole road. "Go ahead," I say. "Take it."

As I park in front of the store, a couple standing off to the right of the building catches my eye. Teenagers—him on a pay phone, smiling, looking at her from time to time, kissing her forehead, pulling her into him—her nestling, under his wing, her thumbs hooked into his belt loops. Makes me wonder about me. I'd been married before, at twenty-four, to a guy that had his own travel agency. That was fun for about a year. I don't miss guys, or dating. Maybe I'd miss it if I didn't feel so tired all the time. I see nice-looking men and I look at them; sometimes I think what it would be like to be with them. But I don't feel like going through all that mess of getting to know them. I think the only thing I miss is being in love. That was a nice feeling. No, hell, it wasn't. Took a lot of energy to be in love. Now, I see young people loving it up in public, fresh in love, like them, and I say, "Ok, for them." It's stupid, kind of, being in love. It makes you act stupid. I think about the garbage truck man, the way he smiled, cocked his head—the way he made me smile—and I catch myself, sitting, holding the keys in my hand, staring at the brick of the building, and laugh.

In one corner of the Quick Stop is a fast food set-up—a Chinese franchise. I've been hungry ever since I smelled the sausage cooking at the drugstore. Figure it's time for brunch, at least. I order Moo Goo Gai Pan, fried rice, a fountain drink. There are four small square tables. I pick the one closest to the checkout counter because there's a TV there, angled just so. I rip the little white fork out of its plastic bag, settle a napkin in my lap, and before I can take a bite, I'm caught up by the pitiful man on the screen, in tears, trying to explain to Maury Povich how he accidentally shot and killed his daughter. I put my fork down and take a couple of swallows of the drink. Forget it—eat, I tell myself. I only eat about a third of what's there—I'm tasting lard. Can't be, I think, but I take another bite, put my fork on the plate and cover the plate with the napkin from my lap.

There's a shot of the grey whales on the TV. I'm wishing the lady there would turn up the volume, but she's staring out at the parking lot. I wonder where they're shooting the shot from because there's not a soul around. The whales are beautiful and there are lots of them and they pitch and roll for the camera. At the end of the clip, two little white words showed at the bottom of the screen, "Siltcoos Beach." I shove the plate toward the center of the table and rest back in my chair with a sigh. I'd driven right by there—fifteen, sixteen miles back. After I pay, I sit in the car trying to decide—back to Siltcoos or on to the Head. The teenage couple is gone. The Head is probably closer now, so might as well check it out first. Traffic's really picking up. Midday—it's typical. I have to wait a minute or two for a break in the steady stream of cars to get back on the highway. I catch an opening behind a black Probe with dark, tinted windows. I'm getting excited now about seeing the whales. Used to beg my parents to take me to see them when I was a kid. Every year they promised they would, but every year we managed to miss them.

A sign reads "Yaquina Head 5 miles." The traffic is getting slower and slower and now, for some reason, we aren't going anywhere. Just stopped. I'm thinking, God, now what?

I wait and wait, stare past the guardrail on the other side of the road, out at the ocean, the top water choppy. There's a wall of white on the horizon—no sky, no ocean, just a wall of white. I put the car in park, kill the engine, and relax into my seat. If I've got to be stuck in traffic, I'm thinking, this is about the best place to be. I turn the radio on, keep it down low—everything seems so quiet. All these cars lined up, all the motors off, not a voice to be heard. I expect it any minute—the great stir of voices to start—from somewhere. I almost wish it would. I close my eyes, and—*whoosh, whoosh*—my hands grab for the steering wheel. I bolt upright just in time to see the back ends of two state trooper cars, lights flashing, but no sirens, and it dawns on me that there isn't any oncoming traffic. Hadn't been since I'd been sitting here.

People are starting to get out of their cars now. Some stand in the oncoming lane, looking forward, bending this way and that, then on tiptoe. Some cross the highway and stand looking out at the view. A woman grabs a little boy's hand about the time I think he's a goner—one more step and he'd have walked right off the edge.

Suddenly, people start making their way back to their cars and engines are starting up. Traffic is moving again, barely. I inch along with the procession, turn the radio up, and smile when I picture the garbage truck man singing this song to me, him standing on the back of his truck, cocking his head the way he would, signaling to the driver to hold up for a minute, me sitting in the shade at the four-way. I picture him jumping off the back of that truck, fussing at the man who flipped me the bird, "Hey you," he'd say. "You want me to dispose of that finger for you?" And he'd pretend he was going to chase after the car, running a bit behind, but he'd stop, and swivel around in the street, laughing, holding his arms high out to his sides, the leather duster flapping gently. Then he'd bow, jump back on his foothold, turn his back to the truck, and smile. That's what he'd do.

We go maybe a mile and now I see what the holdup was—wreckage blocking the entire highway. State troopers are directing us through a scenic lookout on the opposite side of the road when I spot it, the wrecked car, off to my right—the tan Saturn, the Utah plate crushed even with the pavement. It's one of those moments when your senses become extremely acute, and you hear your heart beating and every inch of your skin tingles. I get only a quick look at the car, at the plate. It's still sitting on the right side of the yellow line, crushed like the cars in monster truck shows. I look quickly at the wreckage ahead, truck lying solid on its side, remnants of a forest green dune buggy scattered, trailer at an angle to the truck. I realize I've come to a complete stop, but I can't seem to get my foot off the brake. There's a trooper just ahead of me on my left, jerking his hand harder as if to tell me to hurry up. I look one last time off to my right, at a small group of people standing in front of the Saturn, talking, arms folded or in pockets. No mad rush to get into the car. No fighting to open the doors, or reach through a gap to feel for a pulse or hold a hand. The trooper is starting to walk toward me now, jerking his arm, and I glare at him, thinking wait a goddamn minute—just one goddamn minute. And I look at the car and it's so crushed you can't see inside. The trooper is close now, no longer waving his arm, just walking rapidly. Angry. I ease my foot off the brake and place it on the gas and when the car starts to roll a bit, the trooper slings his arm as if throwing a baseball in the opposite direction. I hit the gas, but then the trooper is in front of the car, with his hand up, signaling me to stop. He's looking in the other direction. I just do hit the brakes in time and the car jerks to a standstill. Idiot! I'm thinking. First you tell me to go, then you jump in front of the car—big mistake.

A rescue vehicle is backing in toward us. It stops in front of us. No, please, I'm thinking, don't do that—back around. Back around to the Saturn there. There's room there. But the two doors open and two men step out. They walk over to the group standing in front of the Saturn, staring at the car, their hands on their hips, nodding, listening. Other rescue people show up, carrying equipment of sorts. Tools, it looks like. There is another rescue worker leaning into the open window of the overturned truck. I hear the sound of hydraulic equipment off to the side. I look at the trooper. He's standing in front of the car, his arms folded, staring at the Saturn.

I think about tomorrow, going back to work. I work at an old folks' home. Fifteen years and most times I feel as old as my patients. I shave old soft faces with electric razors, the droopy skin turning pink, eyes watering and always staring at the ceiling. There's tomato soup to spoon into faces that jerk uncontrollably. Sheets to change—always sheets to change. Old sick people smell. I bathe them, sprinkle powder, tuck them in crisp, white sheets. I open curtains. Smile and talk the sunny talk. Pack up one's belongings—worn out gowns, teeth, brush, old, cheap dimestore jewelry, hair pins. I bring in the new patient, unpack the fresh gowns, new slippers, scented powders. I read to them as they stare, unblinking. I look at their eyes, right up close in their eyes, and I know—they're already someplace else. Fifteen years ago, I felt something for them. I was good at my job. They were all my friends and we'd have long conversations.

I look out to the white wall of the horizon. I see the twins jumping around in the back seat. Were they dressed alike? I wonder. I can't remember. Did I notice? I close my eyes and try to recall their shirts, or the tops of their dresses, or whatever it was they were wearing. They must have been matched. If they weren't I would have noticed. Because twins dress alike. Or maybe not—maybe I wouldn't have noticed unless they *were* dressed alike. But, no, I think, they had to have matched. They do that when they're little. But the sun was in my eyes. I mean it was glaring. I could barely see their faces. When twins are little though, their mothers dress them alike. Don't they? Well, most of them. I glance over to my right—I can't make out what I'm looking at—but there's an arm, a large arm twisted around and a rescue worker with tools hunched over it. Out of the corner of my eye I see the rescue men walking with something to the ambulance.

I stare back at the ocean. The garbage truck man would be raising hell about this. I know. He'd be out there, he'd be doing something. I wonder what he looks like when he's serious. What's he look like when he's staring out at the ocean? He won't smile. No—not that. Nothing cocky. He'd be somber or something. He'd be gentle and his arms would be warm when the breeze blows in off of the water. He'd look at the rocks and his forehead would wrinkle and he'd hold tight. He'd kiss soft at first. I'm sure. Then long and complete, the kind you don't want to end, the kind that carries you into extremes.

Portrait

*I*n Mrs. Richardson's room, Bennie was snapping her fingers, keeping rhythm with the Broadway tune she was humming. She stared at a portrait on the wall. The frame was a dark, red-tinged wood with an inscription that read "Mrs. Elizabeth Jarrell-Richardson." Bennie studied the woman in the portrait. She was a hard one to nail down, at first looking bossy, but the eyes were too soft. Maybe quietly confident. Finally, Bennie decided she wouldn't have liked the woman in the portrait. She looked too uppity.

Across the room, the old woman was lying in a fancy bed. The other residents of the nursing home had standard hospital beds with chrome safety rails that lifted on the sides. But this was the "Richardson Suite" and nothing standard remained. Hers was like a bed you would sleep in at home, a real home. The bedposts were fat and round, reaching shoulder high and made of the same cherry wood as the picture frame. It looked like the bed that Lisa Bradley's father had made for her. Lisa was a girl she knew from school. Her father was always making things for her, things out of wood, and teaching her how to make things. Everyone loved Mr. Bradley. And Lisa.

Bennie looked around the oversized room. It was decked with furnishings all made from cherry wood. There were a bentwood rocker, two nightstands, two dressers with rounded fronts, an unspectacular but wide desk, a grandfather clock in the corner, a carved trunk at the foot of the bed, and a skinny table with legs that met the floor in the shape of paws. The skinny table sat in front of the windows and supported a twenty-gallon aquarium.

Bennie looked from the portrait to the old woman and back again. The mole on her cheek was the only similarity between the two. Bennie had liked the mole on the woman in the portrait. It made her look daring. But age had ruined it, made it big, puffy, and now it just looked like something that needed to be removed.

The woman in the bed was bony and she had that dry, onion-skin look, like she'd bruise or bleed if you touched her hard. Her hair was a fuzzy gray half-inch mess and you could see the pink of her scalp showing through. In the portrait, the hair was a sleek brown, thick, and pulled into some kind of an up-sweep and the skin glowed. Looks French, Bennie thought, even though she wouldn't have known French from Italian, or Russian, or whatever.

The woman stirred, opened her eyes, and stared up at the ceiling. She was surrounded with pillows and covered to the waist with a plump, blue comforter. Her puny body lay on a section of lamb's wool against the bedsores that develop in patients that were bedridden. Money can only do so much, Bennie thought and smiled, feeling suddenly superior to the woman in the portrait.

"Where's my nurse?" the old woman asked. The question, the voice itself, came as a surprise to Bennie. Mrs. Richardson, she had heard, was a "veggie" case, the result of a stroke three months earlier. Bennie walked over and stood beside the bed.

Mrs. Richardson looked at her and asked again, "Where's my nurse?"

"She had to leave, to run some errands or something. She'll be back in a minute. She asked me to sit with you."

There were large blue veins running their courses through the old woman's temples.

"Errands or something. Oh, joy. I pay a nurse twelve hundred dollars a week and she leaves me with a sitter. How much is she paying you?"

Bennie thought sure she could see a pulse in those big veins. "She's not paying me anything. I'm a volunteer, a 'Sunshine Girl,' you know? But, I really didn't volunteer to be a volunteer," Bennie said.

"Explain that, would you?" Mrs. Richardson's eyes were still as soft as they were in the portrait, but the uppityness was showing.

"My mom worked this thing out with the director of the nursing home. I come here every day after school until Mom gets off work to pick me up. Seems I can't be trusted at home alone," Bennie said and walked around the bed to inspect the fish in the aquarium. Just two lonesome fish in one big tank, with a ceramic diver in one corner blowing bubbles from his mask.

"If you can't be trusted, I'm not sure I want you in my room. I have some very expensive, some priceless, knickknacks. I would be quite disturbed if anything should be misplaced."

Bennie walked about the room, touching every priceless knickknack she saw: the gold pen set on the desk, the silver hairbrush on the dresser, a porcelain doll on the nightstand, and crystal figurines scattered about the room. She looked back at Mrs. Richardson, checked to see if she looked worried, and then smiled and said, "You can trust me. I don't steal things and I don't see anything here I want anyway. The thing is," Bennie leaned over the bed, to whisper, "I like to be with men."

"Then you should go fishing with your father."

Mrs. Richardson's answer had come too quick, revealing none of the shock that Bennie had hoped to see.

"My father doesn't fish."

"Oh, well, then of course. What else is one to do? Besides fishing with our fathers what is left for us women except to spend our time *being* with men? So then, you're quite right. You should *be* with men, lots of men, all kinds of men. And right you are to start young. There are so many of them, you see." She squinted her yellow eyes, multiplying the wrinkles that skirted them. "How old are you?"

"Sixteen," Bennie said, watching her eyes, her mouth.

"Oh dear, you should have started much earlier. Your clock is ticking you know. You may have to double up on them, take them by the pairs. Do you think you can do it?" Mrs. Richardson had yet to smile. Her purplish mouth was a little oval with tight wrinkles radiating outwards on her sallow face, like the lips were pulled together with a drawstring.

Bennie giggled and shook her head, "No ma'am. I don't guess I'm ready for doubles."

"Then I shall pray for you child. What is your name? I must know. I will ask God to give you the stamina to catch up, to double up, triple up, if you must."

"My name is Bennie," she said. She felt like a small child and she enjoyed it.

"Bennie, my goodness, isn't it just a perfect name. A man's name. Well, Bennie, I shall pray for you and you, dear, must take vitamins every day and walk, yes, walk at least a mile. Every day.

And you'll see, before long you will have the stamina to take on a whole covey of men."

Bennie was laughing when the nurse came in. The nurse, tall, lanky, and severely flat-chested, put her brown purse down next to the bentwood rocker. She put her hands in the front pockets of her uniform and let her long, monkey-like arms hang limp. With one eye squinting and the other open wide, she stared at Bennie. Bennie looked at the nurse and didn't understand her expression, why she should look so outdone. She gave one last giggle, a stifled one, and looked back at Mrs. Richardson. The old woman stared straight up, without blinking, as if she had just checked out.

"Are you making fun of Mrs. Richardson?" asked the nurse.

Bennie mimicked her, *"No, I'm not making fun of Mrs. Richardson.* We were just talking about men," she said and looked at the old woman with a smile. But Mrs. Richardson acknowledged nothing, only stared like one of the veggie cases. The sunlight from the window, filtering through the water in the aquarium, made it appear foggy. An angelfish hovered near the center and a high-strung scavenger vacuumed the blue and white gravel at the bottom.

The nurse sighed, reached over, and smoothed back the old woman's hair, then roughly pinched her cheek. "Mrs. Richardson can't talk; hasn't been able to say a word since her stroke and I don't find this funny in the least."

Bennie didn't like the nurse. "She does talk, airhead. We just had a whole conversation about screwing men." Bennie leaned over Mrs. Richardson and whispered, "Show her you can talk." But the old woman didn't respond and Bennie saw nothing when she looked in her eyes. There was a red mark on her cheek where she had been pinched.

The nurse hustled around the bed and grabbed Bennie's arm. Squeezing it hard, she started leading her to the door. Bennie, confused, couldn't speak.

"It's a pitiful thing--a girl your age making fun of someone as helpless as Mrs. Richardson. I want you to leave and I don't want you back." The nurse was holding Bennie's arm with one hand and opening the door with the other.

Bennie looked over the nurse's shoulder at Mrs. Richardson. The old woman, looking at them now, winked and smiled. Then she turned into a veggie again.

As Bennie stepped through the door, the nurse said, "I'm going to speak to the director about you."

Bennie caught a glimpse of the portrait on the wall behind the nurse, recognized the soft eyes now and the peachy smile. She grinned and said, "Suck eggs," and walked the long white hall to the lounge. She gathered up her books and purse and went outside to wait for her mother.

Standing by the double doors, she lit a cigarette and stared down at the clean, red mat with a black WELCOME. A gold and white vendor's van pulled up and a short, bald man in a green uniform got out and proceeded to fill the snack machine in the foyer. The traffic had started backing up at the stoplight. Rush hour had begun. She finished her cigarette and lit another. The Frito Lay man slammed the door shut on the snack machine, picked up his empty boxes, and shot her a disapproving look as he walked past her. She smiled, said, "Bye," and watched him drive away. She couldn't figure out why the old woman wouldn't want the nurse to know she could talk. I'll find out one way or another. Maybe I can get her fired.

Her mother pulled up in the sleek, white Lincoln. Bennie mumbled, "Why can't she drive a Volkswagen?" She flicked her cigarette in front of the car, got in saying, "A little white Volkswagen. Yeah, that'd be cool," then shut the heavy door.

"Jesus, Bennie, how do you think that looks? The daughter of the high school principal, sitting out front, where the whole world can see you, smoking a cigarette?" Her mother steered the long car to the exit and looked hopelessly at the line of traffic.

"You worry too much what everybody else thinks. Me—I could give a flip what they think." Bennie shucked her Nikes off without unlacing them and propped one foot on the dashboard. Her mother looked nervous. Her foot danced from the gas pedal to the brake, gas pedal, brake and the car moved only in inches.

A man in a yellow Nissan waved and let them slip out in front of him into the backed-up lane.

"Mom, I need you to do something for me."

"Which is?" Her mother adjusted the rearview mirror, smiled, and waved backwards to the man in the Nissan.

"I'm worried about Mrs. Richardson."

"Elizabeth Richardson? Why?" Her mother's attention perked up at the old woman's name.

"She's a high-risk patient, you know? She needs round- the-clock care."

"Bennie, for God's sake, she has her own private nurse."

"Yeah, well, that nurse is a flake. Leaves poor Mrs. Richardson alone for hours at the time. Honest. I had to sit with her today, a long time. Mrs. Richardson's paying her something like twelve hundred bucks a week. And she leaves her alone like that. It's a rip-off." Bennie looked at her mom. She looked like she was being convinced.

"Well, honey, what can I do?"

"God, Mom, it's obvious. The director is like Dad's best friend."

"Another reason you should not be sitting out front smoking," her mother fired back, then busied herself with trying to get through the light before it changed again. "Still, maybe I'll talk to your father about it."

Bennie sat satisfied. Her mother would make the story even worse than she'd heard it and her father would feel a civic duty to relay the ugly story to Ray Kitchens, the director. Mr. Kitchens, of course, would be obliged to inform Mrs. Richardson's family members and they, no doubt, would axe the nurse.

That evening, as they sat around the supper table, cutting their pork chops and passing the rolls, Bennie asked her father, "Dad? Do you think we could do something really outrageous this weekend? Like go fishing?"

He looked at her mother. They put their forks down, stopped eating, and stared at Bennie. Her father's bald head was dotted with small, black moles, fourteen at last count. He looked down at the table, a serious mood wrinkling his forehead, and began dabbing at the sesame seeds that had fallen from his roll onto the table by his plate. There was silence in the dining room and for a second the light seemed more intense, the way it did during a half-second surge. Then he said, "Well, Bennie, I don't know about this weekend, but we could look into one of those deep-sea fishing trips like Earl Smith is always raving about. If you'd like I could arrange one of those." Having gathered a fingertip full of the seeds he carefully rubbed them off onto the edge of his plate.

"Can't we just find a pond somewhere, dig up some fishing worms, and fish?"

Her father laughed, nodding his head, and said, "Sure, Bennie." Then he and her mother looked at each other and grinned as if to say, "Oh, isn't she adorable," and started eating again. The knives scraped across the china. Her mother dabbed her mouth with a linen napkin and returned it to her lap, and Bennie knew they wouldn't go. I'll have to talk to Mrs. Richardson about this, she thought, and cut her asparagus in two.

The next Wednesday the yearbooks came out. Bennie shoved hers in with her other books, so no one would suspect she was excited about it, and picked a seat in the back of the bus hoping she could glance at it. But Jason Mann dropped down in the seat across the aisle from her so she never even looked at the cover. He had one in his stack of books, too, and he stared out the window while the books sat on the seat beside him.

When the bus took the curve on Trevor Bridge Road, Bennie watched to see if Jason would put his hand out to steady his books. He didn't. They could have spilled over onto the floor of the bus. He didn't look as though he was trying, like Bennie, to be cool about it. He looked like he really didn't care. He has a life, thought Bennie.

The bus stopped at the nursing home and she got out, walked across the parking lot, and went in the side entrance instead of the front. She wanted to get to the lounge and check the yearbook out before she got wrapped up with Bingo. Wednesday was Bingo day. She would have to help get all the old folks into the rec room.

She got a drink out of the machine and sat at the table. She lit another cigarette and ran her fingers over the leather cover of the yearbook. The name embossed on the front felt like braille. She took a drag off her cigarette, set it in the beanbag ashtray, and opened the yearbook to the first glossy page. Turning the pages slowly, she absorbed the faculty, the office workers, then the various clubs.

The pages were full of black and whites taken during school events, everybody in action. The debate team, the prom queen, the Harvest Dance, pep rallies, cookouts, tailgate parties, scoring the basket, sliding in at home base, making a winning touchdown, pyramids of cheerleaders—and one face graced almost every page. Lisa Bradley. Lisa on top of the pyramid, Lisa on the stage in a Cinderella gown, Lisa playing Santa's elf, Lisa riding her horse at home—how the heck did she sneak that one in there? Lisa was on the yearbook committee as well as countless other committees.

This is disgusting, Bennie thought. This is supposed to be one of those important keepsakes to be cherished throughout life, to remember all the cool times twenty years from now. Good ole GCHS, the green and the gold, go Eagles go.

She crushed out her cigarette, and looked at her watch. It was 3:45. Bingo at four. She stuck the yearbook back in the pile with her other books, turned to go, but changed her mind and grabbed it, holding it under her arm, as she headed down the hall. She could get some of her old buddies to put their X in it at the Bingo game.

Ida, the recreational director, stopped her in the hall. "No Bingo today, Bennie. I have to go sit with Mrs. Richardson."

"Why have you got to sit with her? She's got a nurse."

Ida was a short, black woman in her late forties who looked great in jeans and cowboy boots, which is the only thing she ever wore. She had a collection of western shirts to complement the jeans and boots. She was cool.

"I've got to stay with her until the new nurse comes. The old one quit. After ten years of being with her—just up and quits." She reached around and made sure her shirt was tucked just so in her jeans, her huge breasts threatening the buttons, the beaded fringe dancing at the yoke. "Stupid move if you ask me. That old woman hasn't got much time left. The family has probably already ordered her a cherry wood coffin. They might have been real grateful for those ten years of devoted service, you know what I mean?"

Bennie was trying not to grin. "She just up and quit? No one knows why?"

"No one's saying if they do."

Bennie felt important. "I'll sit with her for a little while if you have something else to do. I like her."

"No. Bingo's canceled. I can do it."

"Please, Ida, let me. Just fifteen minutes. I promise I won't touch anything and I'll watch her real close. You can go to the lounge. Relax awhile. Come on. Kitchens isn't here. His car isn't in the parking lot. Just fifteen minutes."

Ida looked at her from the corners of her eyes, thinking. "I'll give you fifteen minutes, but I can't figure why you want to. Don't touch anything."

"I promise. No touching." Bennie hurried to the Richardson suite, pushed the heavy walnut door open and stepped in. She walked to the edge of the bed. Mrs. Richardson's eyes were closed. Bennie walked around the bed as loudly as she could, dropped her yearbook on the floor, and looked to the bed. The old woman had not stirred. Bennie picked up the yearbook and leaned over the bed. "Mrs. Richardson," she whispered.

The eyes opened and Bennie smiled down at her. "Hey, Mrs. Richardson, it's me, Bennie."

"You got my nurse in trouble and you smell like a cigarette factory," she whispered back and her face was stern. Then she closed her eyes, took a deep breath, and said, "God, what I wouldn't do for a cigarette."

"She was an airhead, Mrs. Richardson. She said you couldn't talk."

"She thought I couldn't."

"You made her think that. Why?"

"You're very nosy. But I'll tell you if you promise to sneak me a cigarette next time you come."

Bennie couldn't picture it, but still she nodded.

"I had a series of small strokes," Mrs. Richardson began. "I happened to overhear the doctor explaining to my daughters that he was uncertain if my speech had been affected. I seized the opportunity."

Bennie waited for more. The old woman returned her stare.

"I don't get it."

"Neither do I," she mumbled. "I was sick to death of small talk with my nurse. And I was sick of trying to defend myself. You see, I never was a traditional mother. I was busy. I did not put my life on hold when my daughters were born. Actually, I stopped just long enough to give birth. They want answers I can't give them. They want a mother I can't give them."

Bennie felt compelled to take her side. "Don't you miss talking to people?"

"Not at all. I have ninety-two years' worth of memories and delightful conversations in my mind. I am never bored."

Bennie walked to the aquarium and bent over, looking through the glass. The angelfish was gone. It made her nervous. She turned back and asked, "Why did you talk to me then?"

"You hum Broadway tunes. I used to."

Bennie smiled. "Cool," she said.

"What have you got there?" The old woman pointed to the yearbook.

"Oh, yeah. Just got it today. I want you to sign it." Bennie offered the book to Mrs. Richardson and helped her turn the stiff pages.

"Who is this young man? He's absolutely beautiful." She was pointing to Jason Mann.

"Oh, absolutely. Trouble is, he knows it. He's Jason Mann. King of the green and the gold."

"King of what?"

"Never mind. School colors."

"Oh, yes, well I knew that. My, my, my. This girl must be very important. She's on just about every page," Mrs. Richardson was pointing a crooked pinky at Lisa in the elf suit.

"It's that obvious, huh? I guess you could call her queen of the green and the gold. That's Jason's girlfriend, Lisa Bradley. I hate her."

"Yes, and go right out and cut her throat then. Have no mercy."

"Don't tempt me."

"Then debone her, make some fillets, smoke a ham, cut some stew meat. Looks to be pretty lean meat—very healthy. I don't know about the heart and liver though. I've never been much for that, but I suppose if you smother it in onions and gravy, it might make a pleasant meal."

Bennie giggled again like a child. "Yeah, right, you mean Dahmerize her."

"Beg your pardon?"

"Oh, never mind. I forget you've been out of circulation a while." Bennie was sorry she said it, but Mrs. Richardson didn't seem offended.

"Go to the desk there and bring me my pen."

Bennie walked to the desk and got the gold pen from its velvet nest. She gave it to Mrs. Richardson who scribbled something quickly, slammed the book and handed it back to her. She held the pen out for Bennie to take and at that moment, Ida walked into the room. Bennie grabbed the pen and walked to the desk to put it away. She knew she'd been busted. She looked at Mrs. Richardson and was surprised to see her smiling at Ida.

Ida went to Mrs. Richardson, leaned to kiss her cheek, and said, "You talk to her, huh?"

"Oh yes. She's quite interesting."

Bennie liked that—quite interesting—cool. But she was disappointed that she wasn't the only one that Mrs. Richardson talked to. It had made her feel special, important.

"Well, she has to clear out of here now. Mr. Kitchens is on his way with the new nurse."

Bennie asked, "Is she young?"

"Mercy, no. She's ancient. The family wanted someone old and settled. Now, you gotta go. Go!" She made a fuss with her hands toward the door and Bennie scooted out with her yearbook under her arm.

Back in the lounge, she couldn't wait to see what Mrs. Richardson had written. It was across the top of the page, in a fancy, though shaky, script. "Bennie—In the words of John Ruskin: Remember that the most beautiful things in the world are the most useless; peacocks and lilies, for example. And in the words of Elizabeth Jarrell-Richardson: Lisas come by the hundreds. A Bennie is rare." It was signed, "Liz." Bennie sat reading the words over and over. When her eyes got hot and teary, she gathered her books and went out front to wait for her mother. She lit a cigarette and opened the yearbook again. After reading the words out loud to herself she stuck the yearbook back in with the others. The welcome mat was still clean. Traffic was lining the street again. She saw her mother coming down the street with her turn signal on. Sure would be nice to believe sweet bullshit like that, she thought and flicked her cigarette in front of the car.

Silk

The duct tape does me in. Duct tape has a smell all its own, like something kin to vinyl. And a tackiness like no other tape. The sound of it coming off the roll, though; now that classifies it. *Zhuup. Zhuuuuppp.* You don't forget that sound.

My husband, Joel, is packing up the last of his sister's things to send to her. A year ago we'd bought the house from her when she moved to Connecticut. She'd left one room scattered with stuff she'd meant to come back for. "It's probably just junk anyway," she'd said, calling to ask Joel if he'd sort through it. "Trash the trash, send what you can't bear to throw away." I'd done the sorting; all he had to do was box it up to send off.

The sound of the duct tape rips through the house. He doesn't have a clue what he's doing to me with that tape. It makes it impossible to think. My father is in Parchman, a life sentence, two actually, and his mother, Nanna Vincent, just called to tell me they moved him to a minimum security wing. So, I can call him.

That tape again—*jeez'um*. I grab the black cordless and slip out to the front porch, sit in the wicker rocker. It's illogical that I should feel safe here—in a screened in porch with a door that merely hooks. But my plants are here, all around, and that's a pleasure.

It was after supper and I had just stepped out of the shower when Nanna Vincent's call came. "He wants to talk to you," Nanna had said. "He'd love to see you, too. Who knows—after you talk a few times—who knows."

"I don't know, Nanna," I said. "I have to think about it. I can't promise."

"Just talk to him. You don't know—what harm—" she broke, frustrated.

"Nanna, I'll think about it." I replaced the receiver, and wiped the sweat from my palm.

Call him. This was new. My shoulders knotted, my head throbbed. In court, one psychiatrist said he was temporarily insane. Another decided that my father was not only completely sane, but lucid throughout that evening. And when it was discovered that he'd planned out part of the thing, he was sunk. His journal was found in his desk at the plant. His last entry was a debate with himself over whether he should wake mother up before he shot her, or let her sleep. And he'd decided to wake her. He did more than just wake her. I saw that.

Little Craig, now, he did shoot him in his sleep. And first; before Mother. The shots woke me and I sat up in the bed, listening, wanting to call out. But I couldn't. More shots. I moved, slow, out from under the covers, turned my feet to the floor, and stood, trying to hush my breathing, thinking hard about each step. It was dark; one window that gave no light. But I knew my room in the dark. I moved with small steps toward the window.

The door opened. The light from the hallway came in with my father, gun in his hand.

He steered me backwards to the bed. I grabbed his wrist and pulled his shirt toward me. "Daddy," I whispered, "what is going on?"

"Shhh, now," he whispered. "It's real important you be quiet. And still. You got to be real still and quiet. Got me?" My head was between his hands, the gun pressed there, too, pressed by my ear, my temple, feeling large, but too small, I thought, too small to help us much. He wiped my tears away with his thumbs. "Stay right here," he said. "I'll be right back. Don't move."

I gripped the sheet in my fists, thinking *he'll get shot*. He was gone only for a minute. He closed the door behind him and it got dark again. I heard something, *zhuup, zhuuuupp*, the sound of it right next to me. For a second I could smell it, then it was over my mouth, around my head, and my hands went up to push his away. He squeezed my wrists, "Stop it." It was a hard, sharp whisper. "You gotta be still. And quiet. I know what I'm doing."

He wrapped duct tape around me, forcing my arms down to my sides, then taped my ankles.

"Now look," he said. "I've got to go to Wal-Mart. I'm out of bullets. Your mother couldn't find them. She put them somewhere and I can't find them. I'll be right back. Don't worry about Craig. He fell asleep on the living room floor watching TV." He rested his forehead on top of my head, breathing hard, then said, "Tonya, now stop crying. You'll make yourself sick. You don't want to get sick with that tape over your mouth."

What was left of my childhood could be broken down under three headings: Anikwue, Humes, and Ingram, each the name of an assigned psychologist. My memories are connected with which shrink I had at the time. Anikwue covers stitches in my knee from broken glass, changing schools in sixth grade, and masturbation. Humes was acne, first bra, and more masturbation. Ingram was first date, driver's license, and birth control.

I took my psychologists regular as vitamins, being that it was deemed vital by a judge, only right, and this practice would eat away at the proceeds from selling the house, also deemed necessary by the courts in order to "maintain" me. But, of course, Nanna Vincent maintained me—at least until a child expert testified that Grandma Moore's would serve as a healthier environment. That was probably right.

While my girl friends were taking their bi-weekly piano or ballet lessons, I was busy resisting therapy in offices that always seemed to have too many windows and chairs. But I was the center of attention; I got away with a lot of attitude.

When Dr. Anikwue asked, "Are you leery of people now, Tonya, do you think?" I had said, "No, not really. I feel funny around Nanna sometimes."

"But not your Papa Vincent?"

"No."

"Why just Nanna, do you think?"

I shrugged. "She talks about him. Nobody else talks about him. You do. But not like her."

Dr. Anikwue propped his elbows on the desk, and leaned forwards, his hands rubbing the back of his neck. This he would do when he was about to ask a serious question. So I added, "Nanna looks like him, too. They got the same eyes, same way of holding their hands palm up when they talk. Like this," I showed him. He picked up his pen and wrote on his long yellow pad.

He once asked if I still slept in silk gowns. It had been the long sleeve, silky pink gown of mine that had saved me that night. I had waited until I was sure Daddy was on his way. When I'd heard the garage door humming open, I'd started wiggling. And when I wiggled, the duct tape moved with the gown. I moved around on the bed trying to shift the gown and duct tape upwards. I got off the bed, onto my feet, and shifted over to the bed post. It was about waist high, spindly enough to work underneath the duct tape when I sucked my belly in. It left a dark purplish bruise on my breastbone, but it worked.

I told Anikwue I slept in a t-shirt most nights. But Nanna Vincent had bought me a new silk gown when I moved in with her, to replace the one kept for evidence, the one that showed up in court and in all the local papers, the one I wore when my father would rub my back to help me sleep some nights, the heat from his fingers passing through the flimsy material. There were other nights—nights when he'd come because I'd called out, and he'd lift me in my slippery silk and carry me to sleep between them, he and mother, and their warmth would pour through my thin gown. I'd always had silk gowns.

Anikwue was laid back, middle-age, thinning blond hair, always wore tan corduroys and flannel shirts with the sleeves rolled up near his elbows. He had nice hands, soft looking, steady— they didn't flail this way and that when he conversed the way Dr. Humes' did. When I moved two towns over to live with Grandma Moore, Humes was assigned to me. He was a suit and tie man. I was twelve. He was like a school principal, had that authoritative air.

"I smoke," I told him. "I hate all men. I'll probably kill one someday." Nothing phased him. He was the only shrink who asked me to describe that night. In detail—wanted me "to walk him through that evening." I told him once when I turned thirteen, "You know, Humes. My life ain't no Stephen King novel for you to slobber over." And he'd sat back in his chair, closed his leather bound notebook, put his pretty pen back in the marble holder on his desk, and stared at me. I stared back; it was all a game.

Then he asked, "Tonya, do you feel guilty? That you survived and your mother and brother didn't?" I looked at my hands—thirteen-year-old hands. He waited for an answer. I was stumped. Guilty about living?

"Maybe," I said.

"That's a normal reaction," he started, then went on about how wrong it was to think like that, how self-defeating, etc., the whole while me thinking about the way I had reacted when I found Craig on the floor in the living room, his small head a deflated mess, the tip of his thumb still between his lips, and that's how I knew he was asleep because he only sucked his thumb when he was sleeping, legs curled in his *101 Dalmatians* sleeping bag, and I'd backed out of the room, my hand pushing the duct tape that I'd pulled away from my mouth back up to it then so I could bite into it, the build-up in my neck that I couldn't release—scared I'd end up like that, that was the thing—running to mother's room. And there, I couldn't go in, couldn't go to her to touch her to see if she was still alive, could only stand in the doorway, pulling the duct tape hard around my neck, one monumental "ma" forming on my lips. But not a sound. That I was bound with duct tape like she was, but not like she was, because I had been bound arms and legs linear and she was splayed from the four bed posts, but that I had also been bound made me think of mostly me and how I didn't want that to happen to me, with blood smeared all over her, and I couldn't figure out how it would have gotten smeared like that, and sprayed on the wall beside the bed, literally sprayed is how it looked, and soaked into the sheets. And that's all I thought running through that house and to the neighbors—not *oh God, poor Craig, poor Mamma*, but *me*, I gotta get *me* out of here. And the scream that finally came from me was at the neighbor's door: "*Help me!*"

This I would never tell Humes. It's what they all worked so hard to hear. And there were times when I wanted to tell them, came very close to telling, wanted to get it on the yellow paper and filed away in a metal cabinet and be done with it.

When Humes took a position in another clinic a state away, the ball was tossed to Dr. Ingram. He was old, but once in a while he'd say something brilliant. He seemed to concentrate more on the future and in this we were alike. But one day he said, "Miss Tonya, I'd like for you to start coming to some meetings we have on Thursday nights. Group therapy, sort of. It's a support group for survivors and families of the victims of crime. I guess you fall into both categories, don't you."

I went to one meeting. I was seventeen then—dating guys that asked, "Did your father really kill your mother and brother?" Some would wait until the second or third date to ask. But always by the third, the question surfaced like a balloon released under deep water, sputtering upwards, deflating everything with it. Yet even though I didn't want to talk about it, I thought of my *survivorship* as giving me a special status. Kind of the way I viewed a Vietnam vet. He'd seen things, done things, survived things—all horrible things—I could never imagine. Then I found myself at the meeting of the support group, surrounded by eighteen other people of special status.

In Ingram's office the next week, I said only, "I don't like to think about that many people being affected by heinous crimes, for Christ sake. What do you think that does to my sense of well-being? Here I've been thinking all these years that what happened to me was truly rare and now I see, no, no, this happens every day. I don't think I want to know this."

Ingram stood up and stared out the long window of his office, what he did when he was thinking. I twisted in my seat. He folded his arms and continued to stare out the window.

I sighed, relaxed into the seat, and said, "I don't think that's how to survive, you know? I mean, hell, you live through it once—isn't that enough? It's been seven years for me. Why won't you guys let me move any further away from it?"

That was my last visit to a psychologist. Seven years of therapy and I still believed it was best to leave it alone. Had the court found my father temporarily insane, had *I* thought he was temporarily insane, maybe it would have made sense. Humes, who I'd mistaken for an idiot, had said, "You need to confront the problem." And I'd hollered back at him, "*I* don't have a goddamn problem. *I* got away. Why do you think that's a problem?"

"You're avoiding the issue," he said. "You need to acknowledge what has been done to you and you need to be able to talk about how you feel now about your father."

"This is what I feel, Dr. Humes," I said. "You want to know—here it is. I don't think he would have done it. I don't think he could have killed me. I think he hoped I'd get away."

"Is that what—"

"Wait, see," I scooted to the edge of my seat. "We went to the ocean once when I was about four. It's the earliest part of my life that I remember. I can't remember anything before that. But this is clear. He was taking me out in the surf. I was squealing and holding round his neck for dear life. But this huge wave tumbled us and snatched us apart. I remember the salt stinging my eyes, how it got up my nose and burned, how I flailed my arms and legs about in a panic until Daddy lifted me by my arms. I remember the way my body slapped against him when he grabbed me out and to him. But this, Dr. Humes, this—his arms were shaking. He was trembling for fear of losing me. And he was trembling, too, when he taped me up that night."

It wouldn't have mattered what Humes said next.

Sitting on the porch now, still holding the phone, rubbing my thumb back and forth across the number pad, that so-called evidence feels pretty weak and I wish I'd worked out some kind of clear understanding long ago about how I really feel about my father. I'm thinking it would even be nice if I had someone like Anikwue or Humes or Ingram to sit on this porch beside me and talk to me about it. I can't mention it to Joel. He despises my father. He'd only say something like, "The son of a bitch hurt you enough already. Leave it alone," which is why I fell in love with Joel in the first place. That leave it be attitude.

But there's a door open here and I can't just leave it be. I either have to go through it or shut it.

Joel steps out onto the porch, his hair wet, a towel around his neck. "You gonna sit out here all night?"

"No, babe. I just have to think, you know? Think about calling him."

"No, no—tell me you haven't been out here all this time holding that phone. Tell me my wife would not do that." He unfolds a lawn chair leaning against the front of the house, pulls it close to the wicker rocker, and reaches over to hold my hand. "You can't call a prison this late. So, give it up for tonight, huh?"

"What time is it?"

"Almost midnight. Time for bed."

"You're kidding," I say and twist his wrist around to see his watch.

"Not kidding," he says.

We sit, looking out at this part of our life, the front lawn, the battered mailbox, the Honda Civic we'd just finished paying for, the leaves that need to be raked. He squeezes my hand, stands, pulling me to my feet, saying, "C'mon. Let's go to bed."

But I hold him back. "You go ahead. I'll be there in a minute."

He drops his head to one side and gives a deep sigh. "Tonya, you can't call him tonight. Come to bed."

"I know I can't call this late. I just want to sit here another minute or two. Joel, I have to think. This is very important to me." I put my arms around his neck and hug him close. His arms wrap softly around me and the warmth of them through my gown is almost unbearable. Before he turns to go in, he kisses me lightly on the cheek, then more firmly on my neck, and whispers, "I love you, Tonya." These are words he doesn't take lightly and I shiver.

I'm not so sure about Daddy anymore. Ask me if he could have done it—if he could have killed me like he did Mama and Craig. I would probably just shrug my shoulders. I know I couldn't answer "no." I've spent the last twelve years trying not to think about him and now suddenly, I can't stop, and he's a good father, this one I'm remembering, letting me play doctor on him with my little plastic case of instruments, leaning for a kiss on the forehead after I'd given him a shot, coaching my first soccer games, walking through my childhood with a video camera, rocking little Craig to sleep, making mother laugh. He was always making mother laugh. I've got mother's photo album. It's full of family pictures. And I can't look at them. It's just too damned confusing to look at them, those pictures of that good family, me always somehow juxtaposed with him. *He saved me for last, Christ sake—that's got to mean something.*

I can't comprehend him doing what he did to mother. To Craig. And I think about all the things I'd ask if I called him. I could ask him if he's glad he got caught. Glad he didn't get me. But I wouldn't. Because I know that if I heard his voice it would be like I was ten again. Like nothing ever happened.

I look at the number I've written on the inside of my wrist. I hold the phone firmly and practice dialing the numbers. Over and over I dial until I know them by heart. I let the phone ring once, just to see how it would sound in my ear. My heart throbs in my chest when I hang up, my fingers shake. I'm breathing like a sprinter after a race.

I calm myself, taking a few deep breaths. I hold the phone to my ear and practice talking to him like I'm angry. Because I am angry now, angry that he still has the ability to make my fingers shake and my heart race like it did that night. "You are shit to me. I hope you're suffering, you son of a bitch. You got no right telling Nanna you want me to call. I'd like to talk to my Mama and little Craig, too, you bastard. What's my chance of picking up the phone and hearing them? If you'd had your way, I'd have quit talking twelve years ago." I plop the phone back in my lap. Swipe away a few tears. It sounded convincing as hell, but it didn't feel right. I could never say it. I wrote him a letter once that said something to the same effect, but I never mailed it.

I hold the phone to my ear again and take a different approach. Something flippant. "Nanna said you wanted to talk to me. Well?" I put the phone down. That was easier. But bogus. Just bogus and I couldn't say it either.

I don't think I can be cold with him. No, it wouldn't be anything like that. I'd hear his voice and my heart would melt and I'd grieve—grieve all over again. And I'd say something stupid like "How are you, Daddy? Are you taking care of yourself?" This is how it would be. And after, it would hurt—I'd be shattered.

I'm staring down at the phone in my hand when I hear the first birds of dawn sing. I look up—the sky is light. I run my thumb across the number pad, back and forth. My father's smile flashes in and out of my mind. I grip the phone tighter in my hands, bent over it now, rocking back and forth in the wicker rocker.

I stop rocking. This one last thing I realize: if I were to call my father, before I hung up, I'd tell him I loved him. I've gone over and over this now. This is clear to me. And I know he'd say it to me first. Equally clear. I want to dial the number just to hear him say those words to me. I won't. I will not, because what I don't know is what I'd make of those words when they came from him. It'd be senseless. I slouch back in the rocker. Senseless as sitting all night in a silk gown on a screened-in porch conjuring up phone conversations while Joel sleeps warm in our bed. I tiptoe quietly through the house, and crawl into bed next to Joel. He pulls me against him, his warmth melting into me, and throws a leg over mine, his arm bracing me snugly. Too snugly, I think, and wrench my arms free. I gently shove his leg off of me. He turns onto his other side, his back to me. I turn to him, place my cheek against his back, curl my legs up into the bend of his and with my arm around him, I hold him tight.

"You all right?" he asks in a sleepy slur.

"Yeah. Just tired. Sleep in with me, will you?"

He lifts my hand to his lips, kissing my fingers one at the time. "You gonna call?" he asks, and laces his fingers with mine.

"No need. I know everything I need to know," I say. "And so does he."

Adele X

There had been, Adele thought, a certain something in her affair with her boss, Mr. Hobbs. Not that the satisfaction was physical; it was sloppy lovemaking at best. But there was something in seeing that cultured relic with a goofy, post-orgasmic look on his face. Of course, the thing had fizzled within a month; no gumption in the liaison to begin with. But he had called her "darling" over cocktails, and that she missed.

He was out to lunch with the others now, probably making Vivian laugh, her with her girdled tush. Adele imagined her spilling out of her constraints into the prying hands of Mr. Hobbs. She would be vocal, her with her fat cleavage, forever accented by that gaudy Dior blue topaz necklace, the chain so light it never really hung, just sat nestled on that blushing bosom of hers pushed up to spilling by some outrageously designed brassiere.

"Oo-la-la, oo-la-la," Adele shook her tired 34 B's and swiveled away from her desk. The office empty but for her, she slipped her feet back into her shoes and strolled from desk to desk, peeping at memos, scrawled notes. She gazed through the glass panel of Mr. Hobbs's door at his neat wine-wood desk, the tasteful matted prints hanging precisely, bringing the walls into perfect balance, his useless globe that sat a bit too close to the vertical blinds. "Should have been a lawyer," Adele had said to him one day, "you've got lawyer written all over you." Mr. Hobbs had smiled. "But, darling, I've done just fine in real estate."

Adele turned away now and stepped over to Denton's desk. Only slightly cluttered. A few papers to finish up when he returns from lunch. "Quietly successful Denton," Adele said, and ran her fingertips along the polished edge of his desk. She lowered herself into his chair and settled back. She looked at her own desk, pictured herself working there, as he might. "Plain Adele. Good natured, hard working, unassuming Adele."

She glanced at Vivian's desk, beset with feminine glory, the dry flower arrangement not so subtly appearing there the day after Adele overheard Mr. Hobbs call her darling. It was an ugly arrangement, its mixture of corals and grays oddly combined within an orangey marbled vase, its eucalyptus odorous as throat lozenges.

She stared at her watch; another ten minutes and they'll be coming back from lunch. This was part of her job—keep the office open during lunch hour; then she'd take her own lunch. Of course, this had been Mr. Hobbs's arrangement; it had given them a safe forty-five minutes. Afterward, he would leave, the others would return, and Adele would slip out and meet him at Dockside Restaurant for slow cocktails. Always at the restaurant, she had adored him. He could be quite pleasant to be around; his talk fascinated her. He truly was an elegant man. His tastes truly were refined. He'd talked about his wife, about his new house, of the bother of moving and she'd listened without a tinge of jealousy.

She wanted nothing from him, had asked nothing of him. She'd hadn't wanted anything from the get-go; it was he who had approached her. "Do you have time for coffee?" and when she hadn't answered promptly, "Please, I'd like to get to know you better. I find you very interesting." And so it had begun. He loved his wife in the old, tired way. It was all very comfortable for him at home, she supposed. As for Adele, looking over the table at him, his well-aged face and scattering of grey, his beautiful mouth, quite attractive, and his hands, always warm—that had been enough.

They were friendly still, and there was a charming kind of teasing between them. She'd never been able to figure, though, why he hadn't gone straight for Vivian. He had, instead, oddly, played a bit of a matchmaker between Vivian and Denton, them both being middle-aged divorcees. Denton, however, wasn't smitten with Vivian and this had nourished Adele's delicate ego—the fact that neither of the men had been attracted to Vivian. Now, yes, now the attraction had surfaced, and perhaps, it had always been there, Adele thought, for all she knew about men.

She found it peculiar, though, that Mr. Hobbs no longer concerned himself with discretion. It was quite apparent that he and Vivian were lovers. Perhaps he's getting bold in his old age, Adele thought. It was right that it was over between him and Adele, she knew. His wife, her husband, it wasn't at all fair.

"Oh Christ, don't spoil the day," she said to the ceiling and walked back to her desk, sitting, slipping off her shoes again, but, nevertheless, it settled on her like dew on a spider web, that dull, sticky mood. She stared at the photo of her husband in its cheap wood frame, ran a finger over the clean lipped edge, and thought about how they'd met at a bar an eternity ago. Had she really kissed him before he'd spoken to her? God, she must have been a loon. Her marriage, now so comfortably impotent, wasn't much of a variation from Mr. Hobbs's—her husband, softly spoiling, an ever cushion between herself and the tedious worries of the day. The bills, the cooking, the ridiculous daily errands that consumed precious hours—he took it all upon himself—and then rubbed her calves in the evening, as if she'd been standing on her feet all day. Truly, though, she was the tired wife—wasn't she always tired? And he was constantly feeding her, "Try this," he would say, "taste," and cheese sauce would wake her tongue and warm her throat.

The phone rang on Vivian's desk. Twice. Three times. She should answer it, take a message. Four. Five. Adele waited for a sixth, smiling when it didn't come. Her own phone had sat nestled in silence all morning. Vivian had received at least three calls that morning, and had made at least that many herself. She was in charge of commercial properties. Denton had been on the phone for an hour with one particular call. He handled the upscale, luxury sales, never nervous about a meeting. One sale a month and he could double Adele's commission, even if she made six sales. She took on everything between luxury and commercial, running all over town showing couples with two tots houses they could never afford and when they stopped dreaming, she'd sell them the clean, comfortable number with the fenced-in backyard.

But today, her phone hadn't rung. Have I spoken to anyone today? Anyone at all? The dog, yes, clearly she remembered speaking to the dog, patting it graciously on its wide yellow head. "Be a good boy," she'd said when she left for work.

But her husband, Rob—how had she managed to forget to tell him goodbye? There was always the courtesy of a kiss with their hellos and goodbyes, but, no, this morning, she distinctly recalled now, she'd left him shaving in the bathroom without a word. Did he notice? she wondered. Well, of course he'd noticed; he had to have noticed. And had she spoken to Denton, or Vivian? Mr. Hobbs? How could it be? Had they spoken—had she not noticed—had she absentmindedly mumbled a polite "morning"? She slumped back in her chair.

 Vivian's coarse laugh preceded her through the door, and the three came in, wrapped in conversation, something to do with a tattoo. Adele took her purse out of the bottom drawer of the file cabinet and squeezed past them as they clustered there between Vivian's desk and her own. "Later," she said softly so as not to interrupt their little soiree. Mr. Hobbs was telling them a story of sorts, each absorbed in smiles, obviously not wanting their lunch hour to end. Denton was the only one to acknowledge her leaving, and without taking his eyes off of Mr. Hobbs, waved a slight goodbye. The door closed behind her, sealing in their laughter. Noisy brown leaves scattered along the curb as a van swished by.

She walked from the Welter Building that housed their real estate office to the old drugstore to lunch with the old people. She liked it there, the wooden floors that creaked, the ancient lunch counter with its green swivel stools, the thick, taut vinyl splitting along the edges, the smell of ice cream and toast, and mostly, the fountain drinks with their strong bite of carbonation.

She took a place at the counter beside a heavy, elderly woman who was sipping an orange drink. Adele ordered a ham sandwich on toast and, glancing again at the elderly woman, an orange drink. The woman looked at her and smiled, fingered the top button of her sweater, and said, "I'm waiting for my prescription."

"Oh, yes, well. Sometimes it takes a while, I suppose."

The old woman nodded and looked at the glass of orange drink that the counter attendant set before Adele. "They're good here aren't they?"

"What's that? Oh yes, the drinks. Yes they are." And her sandwich arrived on a saucer, a dill chip toothpicked on top.

When she returned to the office, Denton was in with Mr. Hobbs and Vivian sat staring at his door, smiling.

"What's up?" Adele asked.

"Denton just finalized the Ogden sale," Vivian said. "They're on the phone with the bank to arrange a closing date."

Third one for the month, thought Adele putting her purse back in the file cabinet and the mood closed around her again. The tired wife, she thought, ever and always the tired wife.

A couple in their late twenties came in the door, the man with a toddler on his hip, and looked from Vivian to Adele. Vivian looked away, flipping through a brochure on her desk. Adele said, "Can I help you?" and the man shifted the toddler to his other hip.

"We're looking for a place to rent, something with two bedrooms, not an apartment though. Something where we can have our dog, too. He's a big dog, part lab, but he stays inside cause he's kinda old. I just transferred here from Terrapin. With the mill, you know, and we can't seem to find anything—"

Adele lifted her hand to halt his spiel, and smiled sympathetically, "I'm sorry," she said, "but we don't handle any rental property. Have you tried Coleman's?"

"Coleman's? Where's that?" he asked, and eyed his wife, nodding toward the door. She turned to leave.

"Follow this road out to the City Development Office—it's a big blue brick building on the right—take a right and it'll be two buildings down on the left. There's a sign. You can't miss it."

The man was already backing out the door, nodding, and the child swung his head around, staring solemnly at Adele. "Ok, thanks." The noise of a truck going by rushed in before the door sealed them back in silence. Vivian glanced up from her brochure at Adele. "Everyone's always looking to rent, huh?"

"Wouldn't you? Housing market what it is? Scary to buy right now."

"Shh. Don't say that too loudly around here." She laughed, running her manicured nails along the little wisp of frosted hair that adorned the back of her neck. "Hell, the economy hasn't stopped Denton." Then she stood, walked over to Adele's desk, and leaning with her hands on her knees, just below her snug navy skirt, her heavy bosom threatening the buttons of her blouse, the Dior topaz squeezed in her cleavage, she whispered, "I heard Denton will be leaving us soon. That he's going to open up his own office."

Adele lifted her brows, "Really?"

Vivian nodded, grinning like a dog with a stick in its mouth, "You know what that means?"

Adele leaned her head towards Vivian, again raising her brows, "What?"

"I'll be taking his place," she said and raised her hands to her mouth to smother a giggle.

"Vivian, your specialty is commercial. What on earth do you know about selling private? What makes you think Mr. Hobbs won't give the job to me? After all, I already know private selling."

"Private's a piece of cake compared to commercial. The paperwork's a bit different, yes, but I'm sure Mr. Hobbs can show me what I need to know. It can't be that difficult. And, Adele, you're too good with families. He could never replace you," Vivian said, and returned to her desk to answer her phone.

Adele watched her as she talked on the phone, the way she smiled and nodded, the way she used her hands to elaborate. She'd get the job, thought Adele. And not because she's sleeping with Mr. Hobbs either. She'd get it because she looked it. She acted it. Just like Denton. Adele imagined her in her suburban childhood with her Barbie doll birthdays and sidewalks to skate on and doorbells rung by well-dressed dates that drove shiny quiet cars. Then she broke out in a smile, thinking of her own childhood in the middle of fields, her own private twenty acres of woods, the fantasy worlds she created at the edge of a dam. Vivian could never have lived the freedom that she had lived, could never have known privacy outside the walls of her house. She'd never felt the rumble of an idling tractor through her back, naked under the sun with a lover, the smell of freshly turned dirt filling her nostrils.

"What are you smiling about?" Vivian asked, and Adele came out of her reverie, pointed to a print hanging on the wall, and said, "That picture there reminds me of a horse I once had. But, that horse looks so foolishly proper, with its little English saddle and its polished hooves, its tail bound, for Christ's sake."

Vivian stared up at the picture, "I think it's a nice picture. Very tasteful. Blends well. You don't think?"

"Yes, it looks nice. Nothing wrong with the way it looks. It's just the horse there." Adele looked at Vivian who was staring at the picture quizzically now.

"Never mind," said Adele and started cleaning out her drawer. She hated slow days. She found a piece of gum, removed the wrapper and popped it into her mouth. She missed her horse. In the summers, when the heat was unbearable, she'd ride bareback and the salty sweat of the mare would sting her thighs. That, Adele thought, Vivian had never felt.

She left the building right after Denton—Vivian and Mr. Hobbs staying behind. She'd only shown one house all day to a couple with absolutely no credit it turned out. She'd parked in the security lot across the street—not because she was worried about security, but simply because she'd never learned to parallel park on the street as Denton had. The walk today felt long as she made her way, head down and shoulders stooped; she felt like a sunflower gone to seed. She saw Denton out of the corner of her eye, fumbling with his keys at his car door. She felt him staring, waiting, most likely, for her head to take that casual turn, for her to mumble that insignificant "goodbye," but she wasn't inclined to look at him as she crossed the street, her footsteps, her every movement, every feature, at that moment, plain. She knew it, felt it, and it tired her. There's no use in this today, she thought.

As she stepped up onto the curb, his car pulled past her, him leaning, a definite wave, but she stared at her feet pressed forward in her shoes, and hearing his small foreign car struggle from first to second to third, she smiled and listened for fourth, but it was lost in the sounds of the downtown traffic. She released the smile now—it was a mere trick of the mind—pretending for a second that it didn't matter, that she wasn't the least bit attracted to him. But, climbing into her car, it mattered. He'll ask himself, she thought, "What's wrong with Adele today?" Or maybe not. Maybe that was all in her head, too. Perhaps he thought nothing, or maybe he was simply thinking about the Ogden sale. It had been an easy sale, the property priced for the greatest appeal, the house having belonged to an architect of local interest who was simply bored with his three-year-old design. Denton would make a clean eight thousand off of that deal.

Adele started her car—no little foreign thing that shifted with exotic sounds from gear to gear, but rather it resembled a gift box in shape, a mid-size, automatic, dark green that hummed pleasantly in reverse. It was exactly the kind of car you would expect to see a plain, middle-aged woman step from. She was comfortable with the car, but there were days, mornings actually, when she longed for the spit of a car she had when she was in college. She missed the thrill of shifting hard, yet smoothly, coming off the clutch with perfect timing, passing the drivers who obviously had all day, taking first as far as she dared before shifting into second, the engine pleading before she would shift into third. She rolled the window down and wondered if her husband was starting supper.

Adele and her husband had bought the house on the lake twelve years ago. Adele had liked it at first; it looked so very suburban. It was an old Frank Lloyd Wright imitation with a slanted roof and numerous windows—absolutely functional, everything built in, no wasted space—and also, no personality. Adele had whined about the price, but Rob insisted, "But it's a Frank Lloyd Wright design," and so they'd bought it.

Adele thought she could bear it because of the lake. But the lake she found disappointing. It was the opposite of the house, she thought. Beautiful, yet useless. She swam in it only once, and the bream had pecked at her ankles. It was dead actually. No movement, no yearning pull of the tide, no sand to plant your feet in, no unknown little tidbits stinging her legs through chaotic crashes of waves. No waves. Only ripples and a gentle lapping that annoyed her.

Rob was in the kitchen, stirring something on the stove. She walked to him, pulled up on his shoulder and kissed his cheek. "What's this?" she asked.

He placed the spoon in the spoon rest on the stove and said, "Swiss-sauced fettuccine."

She peered into the pot on the stove, "No meat?" she asked.

"A bit of bacon," he said and then, "What happened to my kiss this morning?"

She smiled and pulled off her shoes, holding one in each hand, "Did you miss it?"

"I did," he said. "I heard your car pull out of the drive and couldn't for the life of me figure out what I'd missed."

"Well, dear, here's one to make up for it," she said and kissed him neatly on the lips.

She turned, saying, "I'm going to change and then come help you."

The bedroom was different from any other room in the house. She'd redecorated it recently, had removed all the heather and mauve and filled the room with cream and the deepest shade of midnight blue. Rob had stood with his forehead wrinkled toward the carpet, saying, "Is that black?"

"No, blue," she insisted. "Blue for Christ's sake, don't you know blue?" She had been pleased with the change, the way the heavy drapes cut out the intruding light. There are just too many windows in this house, she'd complained when they bought it.

Adele pulled her dress over her head and tossed it across the dark paisley comforter of the waterbed. The waterbed had been a therapeutic purchase, meant to ease the pain and stiffness Rob suffered in his shoulders and back. She slipped on a sweatshirt and jeans.

"Come on, now, it's ready," she heard Rob call from the dining room. She took her seat across from him, the plate before her pungent, steaming, promising. She lifted the fork, cold between her fingers. The pasta slithered through the tongs of the fork as she lifted it, and she blew lightly. He sat watching, waiting, and her appetite left her; she didn't want to eat it, she just didn't want to eat. She set the fork down on the plate, "It's hot," she said, smiling and took a sip of her iced tea, swallowing, then another and another, the lemon nipping tart, cleansing her palate, leaving her teeth edgy.

"I'm sorry, Rob. I'm just not hungry. I think I need to relax for a bit." Adele stood then, walked around the table to him, and bent, kissing his cheek. "I'm going to turn the lights on in the garden and poke around out there for a bit. That always relaxes me. I'll eat in a while; I swear."

Rob nodded, took a swallow of his tea, and clearing his throat, said, "Well, it's pretty gruesome out there this time of year."

She turned on the garden lights from the switch by the back door and stepped out. When she'd first started the garden, Rob had asked,

"Why don't you plant out front where everyone will see it? No one will see it here."

"Exactly," she'd said.

She sat on the bottom concrete step—not so gruesome, she thought. The balsam was in its second bloom. It always managed to reseed itself and bloom one last time before winter. The second time around, of course, the plants were shorter, and bloomed much quicker—went to seed much faster. But the colors were always more striking—the white, maroon, fuschia, lavender. Now, she frowned—snails and slugs had discovered the hosta, and the lush green leaves had receded, the little pests drawing off its succulence, making a lacy brown mess of it. The monkey grass had raised stems of black berries that even the birds wouldn't eat, that would fall on the walkway there and be trampled into purple stains. She stepped along the walkway, toeing aside the little berries.

Out toward the lake stood an old misshapen cedar tree, its flaky trunk forever leaning. "Not a tree grows straight around this lake. Why do the trees lean so?" she'd asked Rob, but he'd only shrugged his shoulders, saying, "It's natural, I suppose."

The back door opened behind her and Rob came out, saying, "You know, we should plant some mums. They would brighten things up this time of year. Aren't mums for the fall?"

Adele turned, took a final look at the garden, and said, "Yes, dear, I think they are." She went in, Rob following behind, and sat down, forcing herself to eat.

Rob sat beside her, "I'll go to the nursery tomorrow—pick up some mums if you like. We can plant them on Saturday. It'll be a wonderful way to spend the day. It's good being outside this time of year. I suppose I should buy a new rake, too? The one from last year is about shot."

Adele nodded, smiling, "Yes, I think you probably should." She pushed her plate an inch back on the table, saying, "Really Rob, that was very good, but I'm afraid you piled too much on my plate."

Adele showered and climbed into bed, Rob waiting, the waterbed jolting swirls under her weight. She lay on her side as she did every night, Rob curling around her, an arm pulling her in, the movement of the bed tapering now to a gentle rocking. But I don't want to be rocked, Adele screamed in her head.

At work the next day, Mr. Hobbs walked out of his office, a pretty smile on his face. He leaned over Adele, his hands on her desk, saying, "Listen, darling," and Adele knew Vivian was watching, listening, "I've asked Denton to show you around his properties. I'd like for you to be familiar with them, just in case anything happens to him," and he lifted himself straight, exchanging smiles with Denton. Vivian was glaring—that's the exact word, glaring—and it was the first time Mr. Hobbs had called Adele darling since he set the ugly flower arrangement on Vivian's desk.

"Of course, Mr. Hobbs, but are you sure you wouldn't want Vivian to go?"

"Vivian?" he laughed, "Darling, you know damn well Vivian doesn't know a damn thing about private sales." Then he turned to look at Vivian, adding, "Of course, she's good at other things. Commercial properties and such." Vivian continued to glare, but it didn't seem to bother Mr. Hobbs. He turned back to Adele and said, "Now then, why don't you and Denton use your time wisely. You could probably see everything in one day, I would think."

Adele grabbed her purse out of the file cabinet and followed Denton outside. Walking towards the car, Denton said, "You know don't you?"

"What? That you're leaving us?" Adele asked.

"No, no. I mean, yes, I am leaving, but I mean them. You know as soon as we leave, he'll lock the front door and—yes, you know. I can tell by that smile."

Adele laughed, "I don't know any such thing. Vivian looked pretty angry when we walked out of there."

Denton unlocked the passenger door of the car for her, but she opened it herself. "She'll give," he said. "She always gives Hobbs everything he wants."

As Denton drove through the downtown streets, Adele felt certain she looked an oddity in the car. She put on her sunglasses and smiled as he shifted the gears.

"Do you want to see the Ogden place?" Denton asked.

"Well, there's really no use, is there? I mean, it's a done deal, right?" Adele said and studied Denton as he drove. He looked so damned comfortable with himself. He had the visage of an ancient Roman, she thought, and she could picture him a naked statue, a wreath about his head, leaning on a sword.

"Just thought you might like to see it. It's pretty damn nice. Nicer than the others."

Adele thought for a moment. "All right. Yes, I'd like to see it," she said.

They took the great tour of the Ogden estate with its enormous wooden beams, the wide staircase with the carved banister, the ridiculously oversized kitchen with its clay tile floors, and skylights. "Impossible to heat," said Adele.

"No, actually, quite efficient. Solar," said Denton. "Do you want to see the rest? The grounds maybe?"

Adele laughed, "No, really Denton, you've already sold this place and I'm afraid it only depresses me."

He took a step towards her, his face turning slightly serious, "Why in the world would it depress you?"

She turned and walked into a great open room, thickly carpeted off-white. "It's so damned grand," she said and then turned back to look at him, saying, "But, I must admit. You look very much at home in a place like this. It suits you."

He smiled and was quiet for a moment and then said, "Tell me. If I make a pass at you, would you tell your husband?"

Adele looked at him, caught a bit off guard, but found him more amusing than serious, "I can't believe you put any thought into that question," she laughed. "I mean, my God, it must have come off the top of your head rather suddenly."

Denton smiled, "Yes, I suppose it does sound ridiculous, but I wouldn't want someone's husband running after me, now would I?" He took a few steps more toward her.

She didn't move, only stood nervous now, trying to think. What was there to think about, for God's sake? she asked herself. She'd slept with Mr. Hobbs hadn't she and she hadn't even been attracted to him. What was there to think about? Something, she answered herself as Denton reached out to take her hand. Surely, there must be something I should be thinking about.

Trespass

In a snip of life, I was as big as ever I have been—real, integral—an integer as opposed to a fraction—yes, that's it. How ironic, then, that my becoming whole so fractured all else.

We lived in the new development of Leverton Heights, a place thriving with middle-class families struggling to live above their means in fine, but overpriced houses on tiny green lots with swimming pools for back yards, settled along smooth, black, sunny streets. Twice a week for four months I had left my nine-year-old son in the charge of my sixteen-year-old daughter and driven across town to take piano lessons at the home of an old German woman by the name of Mrs. Stinger. I did this for myself. I had taken lessons as a child, played the piano for ten years, could actually play quite well by uncultured standards, but then swore I'd never touch one again during a brief but snappy argument with my mother.

Twenty years later, mother died and the piano was moved into the living room of my new house, a pretty thing to look at, polished and lovely with a silk flower arrangement just so on top. I pulled an old music book from out of the piano bench, propped it open, placed my fingers above the keys, and clumsily realized I had not retained the talent. The right hand recalled a few notes and chords of youth. But I was bewildered as to what to do with the left hand. The kids sat on the couch biting their nails, watching, waiting for the moment to end so they could return to the den and watch television. I leaned in closer and closer to the music spread before me, squinting finally, but could make no sense of the bottom chords. The loss cut a jagged path through me, somehow connected with the loss of my mother—a dear, dear woman after all—and my husband squeezed my shoulders as I slumped over the piano and said, "You know, there's an old widow woman that teaches piano across town. A few lessons might be all you need." And so began my lessons.

There was a short cut from Leverton Heights to Mrs. Stinger's house, a road the name of which I never noticed, but it would get me to Mrs. Stinger's a minute quicker than the safer route by cutting through a dilapidated downtown district. This was the old downtown, now abandoned except for the abandoned themselves, though a small nightclub and an even smaller tattoo parlor, both with blacked out window fronts, seemed to remain lively in the midst of several larger condemned buildings. Two minutes out of old downtown, the road led straight to Mrs. Stinger's neighborhood, a place beginning its own sort of decline, offering nothing with which to entice restoration of the dozen or so nondescript brick two story homes whose occupants were as old as their dwellings. Even the sun found not much welcome, having to slip through giant hickory trees that umbrella three entire blocks. The shade, however, I found enjoyable.

I always knocked on Mrs. Stinger's side door with feelings of reverence; I'm just not sure what it was I revered. But there was something in that neighborhood, in that house, missing from Leverton Heights and my house. On the last day that I went there with the intention of actually taking piano lessons, for there would come other days and other intentions, Mrs. Stinger did not open the door when I knocked. I knocked again, and waited, watching across the street as an elderly woman, bent forward at the waist, holding to the seat of a slat back chair as if it were a walker, made her way down her cracked cement drive toward her mailbox. The woman craned her neck, looking around, and spied me staring. I looked away and knocked again on Mrs. Stinger's door.

"She's not here," came a man's voice from behind the tall wooden privacy fence that wrapped the backyard.

"Oh," I said to the fence and stood, unmoved, pondering the situation. "Shall I wait for her, do you think?" I asked. "I mean, for my piano lesson. I'm sure I'm right on time."

The gate opened outward from the fence and the man appeared, a most unusual looking man, a very large man indeed, tall that is, and broad, but not at all fat. A man the size of a large wrestler, his head completely bald, but there was that one thing odd that I couldn't put my finger on, something that gave him a rare look about him, something that had to do with his skin I was certain, but it wasn't that it was too light or too dark or jaundiced or flushed. No, but there was something that captured my attention and made me stare. For sure, he was too young to be naturally bald. I had him by at least five years.

"She won't be here today." He was staring, too, and we had one of those unique, absolutely comfortable meeting of the eyes, and he smiled. "I'm her son, Otto. I'm supposed to let all her students know she won't be here for a while. Her sister in Iowa—cancer, you know?"

"Oh, poor thing. Well, then, I understand, yes, I completely understand, so when you hear from her, please tell her my thoughts are with her." I turned toward the car, took a few steps, then turned back and said, "Nice meeting you, Otto. I suppose she'll call when—well, after. When she can?"

"Yes, I'm sure. But look," he walked a few steps toward me, "since you've got time, you want to see something?" He smiled cleverly.

The question was much too general.

"I found something," he continued, "something sort of interesting in the backyard, here." He pointed to the fence and started backing toward the gate.

I looked about, saw the old woman across the road making her way back up her driveway with her chair, her pace worrisomely slow. Otto disappeared through the gate. Peeking in, I could see an extended cement patio with plants arranged in small, brightly colored pails, none blooming, merely an assortment of greenery. I stopped just inside the gate. "What? What is it? What have you found?" I took another step. This is silly, I thought. "Hello?"

Just then, Otto appeared from behind a large bush off to the left of the gate. He rose from a stooped position, lifting a rather large tortoise. The shell must have been fifteen inches across, a golden brown color with the usual geometric patterning. The head strained out on a long wrinkly neck and the flippers were paddling air.

"Oh my goodness, look at this," I said. "I thought they pulled into their shells when you did that."

"Did what?" Otto's arms bulged tight against the sleeves of his oxford shirt as he turned the heavy tortoise this way and that.

"When you lift them. Or just touch them at all, really."

"He did at first, but I've been playing around with him for about an hour now. He's used to me, I guess. Dug himself up under this fence, I suppose, though I can't seem to find where." Otto put the tortoise on the ground between us and glanced over the circumference of the fence. I knelt with one jeaned knee on the grass and watched the tortoise lift its shell an inch from the ground and begin moving. It had actual claws on the ends of its flippers and its back legs were fashioned much like an elephant's. Even its tiny whip of a tail was similar to an elephant's.

Otto knelt also with one knee in the grass, leaning back on the heel of his boot. "What do you think?"

I smiled and said nothing, just watched the tortoise's sure progress. Otto picked it up and put it back in its starting position.

"You're the woman that home schools her kids, aren't you?" Otto asked, no longer watching the tortoise as I had been.

"Yes, I am," I said. "I suppose your mother told you."

"Well," he knocked his knuckles lightly on the tortoise. It retreated into its shell. "She just said some woman was coming by to take lessons today, for me to be here to explain things, she couldn't remember your name, just referred to you as that woman that home schools her kids."

"Ahhh. Yes." I stood.

Otto stood. "She doesn't care much for you, you know." He was smiling.

"Why on earth not?" I asked, my neck growing warm.

"She has this idea that you take lessons just so you can go home and teach your kids the same lessons. In other words, she thinks you're trying to get three for the price of one." He put his hands on his hips and again, I was taken with the rare quality of his skin, but couldn't define it.

"She's very smart, your mother."

"So you are, then." Otto said, grinning.

"So no, I am not. But still, it is a good idea."

Again, we had a comfortable meeting of the eyes, and his were a soft blue. We watched the tortoise manipulate the world around him. Then Otto looked at me as if he were brooding over a problem.

"Watch," he said, and carried the tortoise to the center of the cement patio, flipped it over, setting it upside down on the concrete. The tortoise again pulled into its shell. Otto looked at me, weighing my reaction. I stopped smiling. Using both hands, he set the tortoise spinning rapidly.

"God no," I said and reached toward the poor spinning tortoise. Otto grabbed my wrists and held them in front of him with one hand, watching me watch it. He kept the tortoise spinning with his other hand, spinning it faster and faster.

"What do you feel for it now?" he asked intently, his face close.

I let my eyes meet his—no hard edges.

"Please stop it—let it up—please," I whispered.

His grip on my wrists softened, but he didn't let me go and he reached down and spun the tortoise even more violently. "What do you feel?" He stared at me as if I might stumble upon the answer to world peace.

"What do you want me to say? Please stop it. It's cruel."

He spun the tortoise so hard that it skittered on the concrete. I searched Otto's face for an explanation. He shook his head and sighed. He closed his eyes and leaned his forehead to touch my fists, then tapped my fists twice against his chest. "A minute ago you thought the tortoise was what? Cute? Interesting?" He spoke calmly. "And now—now you care. You take it seriously. Now you care. See?" Slowly, Otto released my wrists. He seemed exhausted.

I was staring at him dumbfounded. I felt like I should thank him, for Christ's sake. But, of course, that would have been insane. He returned the tortoise to its upright position in the grass. It sat there. Otto pulled up a webbed lawn chair and offered it to me. I sat. I waited for the tortoise to come out. Otto did not sit. He stood behind me. He lifted my hair into a ponytail and held it in his hand. "You have healthy hair. It's nice," he said. I watched for some sign of life from the tortoise. Otto put his large hands on my shoulders, then scrolled down to where my wrists lay on the metal hand rests of the chair. I thought to put my hands in my lap, but he curled his fingers around my wrists and held them in place there. The tip of the tortoise's head emerged, then one flipper. Two. I sighed. Otto moved his hands back to my shoulders, his fingers reaching forward to rub my throat.

"Relax," he said and his voice was soothing.

The tortoise took a tenuous step.

"You see, all is well with the tortoise," Otto said, and gathered my hair to fall across one shoulder, bending to touch his lips to my neck.

"You will come back Thursday? Just as if you were going to have a piano lesson? I can expect you? Please don't lie to me. Yes, you will come. Or no, you will not come." He suckled my neck. My fingers found the rounded edges of the arm rests.

Eyes closed, I nodded yes.

I spent the following day, Wednesday, stupefied. I refused to question any of it, my involvement with Otto, gave the kids the day off from home schooling, spent hours in the ritual of grooming myself for the next day, looking nervously in the full length mirror. When my husband came home, we went out to eat, a place called Dockside on the lake. We ate in silence, then sipped wine until we grew sleepy. He would be leaving for two weeks the following morning. He watched me thoughtfully as I spoke, held my hand as we walked to the car, caught me up from behind and wrapped his arms around me, holding me, rocking gently. I lay my head back on his shoulder, closed my eyes, and listened to the sound of a single boat out on the lake.

"I will miss you horribly, you know," he whispered in my ear.

I never thought Otto malicious, or dangerous. It was not about that. Even when he was holding my wrists in his grip, I was not afraid of him. He did not make me feel helpless. In fact, I felt bold. Somehow stronger. More vital.

I knocked on Mrs. Stinger's door Thursday as I had done every Tuesday and Thursday for months. Otto opened the door with great charm, ushering me through the foyer and into the piano room.

"Ready for your lesson?" he asked and patted the piano bench. I settled on the bench and he sat in Mrs. Stinger's straight back chair beside it.

"You've forgotten to bring your music," he said. "Well, this will do." He chose a complicated selection from the shelf beside the piano. "All right, then. You may begin," he said, and tapped the music in front of me rudely with a pencil.

I played along, spreading my fingers to reach awkward chords and horrendous flats. "Is that right? So far?" I asked. "Is that okay?" The game amused me.

"Well, it can't be, I hope," he said and tossed the pencil over his shoulder. "That's the ugliest thing I've ever heard." He smiled and ran his fingertips along the underside of my forearm. "I'm sorry. I don't read music," he said, and brought my hand to his mouth, touching his lips to my palm.

"I play by ear," he said, and nipped the inside of my wrists with his teeth. Then, of a sudden, he stood and motioned for me to stand. "Exchange seats with me. I'll demonstrate."

The music was new to me. I wondered if he was making it all up, but every note fit the next, and his fingers worked the keys, building then tapering, his eyes on me, the room darkened by thick drapery, and only the two crystal lamps on each side of the piano giving light. This gift he had was amazing, the knowing of the music intuitively. He ended at last and let his fingers slip from the keys. He hung his head and stared at his hands.

"Why is it that you shave your head?" I asked and reached to touch it with the back of my fingers.

He leaned his arms on the music rest of the piano and laid his head on them, looking at me sideways. "I don't," he said. "I have a condition. In fact, if you'll look closely enough, I have no hair anywhere on my body. A genetic disorder."

My fingers stroked his face and it was as a child's. He had no eyebrows, but his eyes were so deeply set and strong that I hadn't noticed specifically, though this did explain the rare quality I hadn't been able to define. Had he not been as tall and as muscular, he would have probably looked somewhat effeminate.

I trailed my fingers over the back of his shirt, admiring the solidness beneath. He stood, stared somberly, and I couldn't imagine what made the man so sad. He walked around behind me, and across the piano room to a settee in the darkened corner. He smiled. I walked over, invited by his smile, and he wrapped his arms around my hips, pressing his face against my waist. His arms trembled and he didn't move, just held me that way. I stroked his head, and rubbed his shoulders, then bent to feel his massive back under my hands. He released me, then pulled me onto his lap, and held me to him again, his face resting against my breasts.

"What is it?" I asked. "What is wrong?"

He looked at me before he kissed me, that strangely searching look that sometimes comes before a kiss, and when he moved beneath me, I could feel him hard. Our lips touched delicately, and then joined in equal aggression, him relaxing now, suddenly seeming to know what to do with me, and the kiss trailed off into him tenderly biting my bottom lip. His tongue followed the line of my neck as his fingers worked the buttons on my shirt. Odd that I'd worn my husband's shirt, but it was this moment that I had hoped for, this unbuttoning, one slow step at a time. He freed my breasts from the cups of my bra, and winced, hungry to suck one nipple, then the other and I pressed myself to the heat of his face, his breath. He moved to look at me and I , him and we smiled. I stood, slipped out of my shoes and he roughly grabbed the waistline of my jeans, jerking my body back to him. I stepped away and out of the rest of my clothes while he stood and undressed. He was beautiful, his muscles clearly defined and his skin, his hairless skin, soft yet solid next to mine. He maneuvered me onto my back on the settee, and we looked at each other as he settled himself above me. He kissed my throat and his hand reached between my legs. I thrilled at the newness of the touch, the fingers foreign to me, their movements unpredictable, unexpected. I spread my legs for him to enter. Again, his arms began to tremble and he held himself still inside me.

"Christ god, be still," he whispered.

I lay motionless beneath him, listening to him breath and sigh against my ear, feeling the beating in his chest. He lifted his weight, kissed my eyelids closed, then the tip of my nose, and shoving himself further inside me, pressed his lips finally to my forehead, grunted and buried his head beside me in the pillow of the settee, moving now, not able to stop. And his moment came and subsided and I was simply in awe of it all, in awe of the complete and brutal way the moment had him in its grip.

"I am sorry," he whispered in my ear.

"No, I'm not. Not at all," I whispered back.

"Next time," he said.

"Yes," I said. I ran my fingers along his spine. "Next time." Silently, I hoped it would be all the same.

I limited the kid's home schooling hours to a mere one hour a day in the mornings. It was simply impossible to think of anything else except the last time I'd been with Otto, or the next time I would get to see Otto. My roles as wife and mother suddenly felt benign, things practiced and rehearsed. My time with Otto was pure earsong. I began slipping out at night after the kids went to sleep. I wanted to make the most of the time that my husband was out of town. I dreaded the limitations his return would bring.

Otto proved to be such a special man. Every encounter began with his music awakening the grim little piano room. But most special about Otto was his ability to see auras and it was this that made him sometimes look so sad.

"What exactly is it that you do, Otto?" I asked once.

"I own the House of Aura," he said.

"What do you do there? I've never heard of it."

"I sketch people and their auras. I take Kirlian photographs. Sometimes I'll do a portrait." He watched closely my reaction.

"Otto, jeeze, you aren't one of those New Age, pseudo science fanatics, are you? I mean, aren't you a little old for such?"

"I see auras," he said quietly. "I see yours now. I see yours always."

I nodded and chewed my bottom lip. I needed to hear more.

"I've seen doctors, had a thousand tests. They tell me they cannot see what they are sure is there—some growth or problem with the occipital lobe. And I tell them I can see what they are sure is not there—for me, they are there. My reasoning is as sound as theirs, it would seem to me." He touched his index finger to my nose, then leaned to kiss me quick. "I don't know what they are. Whatever they are, they are beautiful to me. Sometimes too beautiful."

And you can see mine?" I said, sitting a bit straighter in front of him.

"Yours," he said, "is painfully lovely."

"I want to see what you see when you look at me."

"My sketches are crude."

"Still, I want one."

"When is your mother coming back, Otto? Have you heard?" I was curled around his solid body, a quilt tangled around us on the carpet, his chest rising and falling under my head. It was two in the morning and I didn't want to go home.

He shrugged and said, "She says that my aunt must have a very strong will."

I closed my eyes, yet dared not fall asleep. "Maybe tomorrow you can sketch my aura," I said.

"When you leave your husband and come live with me, I will sketch you. Otherwise, a sketch of you by me is too much evidence for any husband." He worked his fingers through my hair.

"Otto," I said, lifting myself away from him. "I can't leave my husband."

Otto looked at me quickly, then at the ceiling. He rested his arm across his eyes and clenched his fist.

"Otto, you can't think that. I cannot leave my husband. He has given me absolutely no reason to leave him—don't you see, Otto?"

Otto bolted into a sitting position, and beat his fist hard once against his chest. "I—me—I have given you reason to leave him!" He stared hard, breathing heavily. He took my hands, and said quietly, "Haven't I?"

I pulled my hands gently free of him, shaking my head slowly, deliberately, frowning over his confusion.

"Go home, then," Otto said, his voice catching. "Go home and do not come back."

I knew before he said it what it was he was going to say. I was already dressing to leave.

I drove away from Mrs. Stinger's house, through the streets bordered by hickory trees, leaving some enviable part of me behind with Otto. I grieved the loss, my eyes blurring with tears, not caring particularly if I crashed that moment or the next, not caring if I ever made it home. So deeply was I mourning that I barely noticed the gathering on both sides of the street just outside the nightclub in the old downtown district. I slowed at first, to let a few stumbling pedestrians cross, my attention drawn toward the reflection of lights off of the blacked out glass of the small nightclub, the hard bass rhythm of music pumping through the open door.

And then, never had I seen the likes of it, the commotion in front, behind, all around me, my Civic pommelled, black fists banging every inch, nobody caring who was in it, just angry black faces sputtering over top of it at other angry black faces and shaking bandanas in the air, spitting on the windshield, and not another vehicle in sight, not another white face in sight. They didn't want me there and I didn't want to be there, but the crowd in front wouldn't move away, wouldn't open a path for my runt of a car to pass through. I stared, pleadingly, at the furious face that loomed at the passenger side window, and he kicked the side of the car, "What you staring at bitch? Get the fuck off. Carry your white ass down the road, no comprende stupido?" I looked straight ahead at the crowd in front of me yelling, taunting me, "Come on, bitch!"

They grabbed the front bumper, rocking the car, yelling, cursing, till I couldn't make out what they were saying. They were all over the hood and pressing into one another in front of me and there was clearly nowhere to go and in my rear view mirror the crowd was thick all down the street and I don't know how I got in the middle of it, but there was no moving, it was insane to think one could move. I looked back to the passenger side window and a hand with long red fingernails was jerking off some guy, his dick pressing over and over against the window. His words I could clearly distinguish from all the others, "Yeah, you want some of this? C'mon and get you some of this," and I knew damn well it was him banging his fist rhythmically against the roof of the car, humping my car, no less.

My hands had not changed their grip on the steering wheel and my foot was planted on the brake, my leg trembling out of control, *jesus, let me out, let me out,* and then the sharp tap, tap on the window beside me, a fucking gun pointed at me, "Move it bitch. Now," and the words combed the air, honeysuckle thick, "Move bitch!" a chanting monotone command coming from every moving mouth, and the thumb cocked the gun in the window beside my head, my foot slid from the brake, barely perceived the gas pedal, my eyes closed, *fuck you then, just fuck you, be stupid, then, just be this fucking stupid, fucking idiots,* and I opened my eyes and clenched my jaw, and they peeled back from the street as I stomped the gas, humming loudly to myself to shut them out, the shouting and the noise I didn't want to hear if my car caught a body.

When I came loose of them, I looked in the rear view mirror, shaking off tears like a school kid whose been teased hard on the bus, and not one was looking after me that I could tell, but they had closed the gap that was me in the Civic. I beat the steering wheel with my fist and then into the street runs a black kid, just a kid, in my headlights, the hard thump and then over the hood, up against the windshield, a cheek, a hand, then off the side and of course my foot is on the brake, had nailed the brakes, squealing before the hard thump, and in the rear view mirror, they are coming, past one streetlight, then two, then three before I even get out of the car.

The boy was ten feet back, motionless in the road. I ran, knelt beside him, *oh god, oh god,* blood dripping from his nose, and the thunderous rapping of a hundred feet hitting the pavement in anger was too much to bear and I looked at them coming down on me and thought for a split second that I hear sirens in the distance, but at such distance as to be useless to me and readied myself to run back to the car, when the child on the pavement moved beneath me, and I saw too late the glimmer of knife in his hand as it slashed upwards and across my throat. My hand clamped there, yet the blood warmed my chest, as the child jumped to his feel and the crowd lifted him up, "I did it! I did it! I got the white bitch!" and the sound of the sirens was unmistakable now and the crowd began to run in a hundred different directions, and my forehead met the street.

It could have been part of a dream, the voices in my awakening.

"What was she thinking?"

"Mom, I'm sure she'll have answers when she wakes."

"How do you answer for being out at that time of night in such a place?"

"Mom—"

"How do you leave your children at home to go off that time of night? Tell me what answers she could possibly have?"

Silence.

"Your own daughter told you she had done it before, 'a couple of times before,' is what she said."

Silence.

"Well, you may be fool enough to believe her, son. But not me. It would have been better had she bled to death on that street."

I refused to open my eyes to the voices. I could have.

How close he must be, I thought, and she—she must have left—but how close he must have been for the sounds of his breathing to come through to me, the smell of his cologne, a hard, clean, immaculate sort of smell. And how odd that he was so close and yet we were in two separate worlds, him standing there, pacing there. And I wondered what he thought he saw, looking at me, my shut face, me dead to him, yet so alive in this skin. He would never see into the place I was, could never feel what I had felt, could not know what I now know, this world of stained smells, of darkness and light combined, a place thick and full and consuming. Even now, as he stands so close, so separate are we that I can do this, think this, relish this—I can return to the darkness, to night, to the cool air and the gasoline smell of that place—the old downtown—the place I crossed every other day for weeks and returning, I can press my face against the cold blacked out glass, and close my eyes and wait my welcome, the moment the door opens and I'm pulled into the lights, the crush of music new and hard and wonderful to me, the liquor poured warm down my throat, the bite of lime, a warm body so close behind me, holding that mere inch between us, matching sway for sway, allowing a slight brush, breath held, breathing through my skin it seems, my arms wide open in this crowded place, a place of rough black hands and beautiful broad necks, all reaching out for me, enveloping me, and I, trembling, plan the moment of my giving.